# THE DUKE DEAL

## THE WHITMORELAND SERIES
### BOOK ONE

## VALERIE BOWMAN

JUNE THIRD ENTERPRISES, LLC

The Duke Deal, copyright © 2023 by June Third Enterprises, LLC.

Print edition ISBN: 978-1-7368417-7-8

Digital edition ISBN: 978-1-7368417-6-1

Book Cover Design © Lyndsey Llewellen at Llewellen Designs.

*For the incomparable Judith McNaught, whose books have given me countless hours of delight.*

**The honeymoon is over...**

When Veronica said "I do" to Sebastian Sinclair, Duke of Edgefield, she thought all her dreams had come true. He was dashing and doting, and she absolutely adored him—until he betrayed her trust, shattering their marriage, and her heart, into a million tiny bits. She hasn't seen her husband in the two years since, and she'd just as soon make it twenty. But when she learns that her beloved grandfather's dying wish is for her and Sebastian to attend the family's Christmastide celebration, she swallows her pride and asks him a favor: to pretend they're the happy couple they once were.

**But the passion still simmers.**

Sebastian is shocked to find his lovely duchess on his doorstep, but he's ready and willing to play the part of a devoted husband for the Christmas season...if Veronica will grant him a favor in return. All he asks is that she share his bed every night. All night. And maybe even give him the heir he needs.

**Could their love be the real deal?**

Veronica must be mad to agree—especially since Sebastian seems intent on using every weapon in his arsenal to charm and seduce her. She knows it's just pretend and yet, she can't help but wonder if the falling snow and Christmas cheer will work a little magic. Maybe she and Sebastian will end up with more than either of them bargained for...

# CHAPTER ONE

*Essex, December 1814, The Duke of Edgefield's Country Estate*

"Your grandfather is dying."

The words slashed across Veronica Sinclair's heart. She stared at her mother, who had just delivered the unwelcome news. Mama's eyes were red-rimmed, and she looked as if she hadn't slept in days. Had she lost weight? Poor, dear Mama. This must be excruciating for her.

Veronica took a shaky breath. Despite the ache in her chest, she had to be strong. Mama needed her. "What do the doctors say? How much time?"

Mama lifted her chin, but Veronica could see the pain in her eyes. Her stoic, perfectly mannered mother was at her limit. Mama's father, the esteemed Duke of Holden, was dying. That a man, so vital and powerful, was nearing the end of his life, defied belief.

"Not much," Mama finally managed, her voice reed thin. "I merely hope he'll live through Christmastide at Whitmore Manor."

Veronica swallowed hard and nodded. Christmastide had always been Grandpapa's favorite time of year. Christmas Day was next week. And Whitmore Manor was where her grandfather resided now, to spend time with Mama.

Grandfather was a duke, and Mama herself was a marchioness. She'd married Veronica's father, the Marquess of Whitmore, when she was a girl of nineteen. Together they had raised four children before Father's death seven years ago. Veronica, the eldest of the three sisters, had married a duke. *Edgefield.* Yet Veronica hadn't wanted to marry so young. She'd wanted to ensure she made the best match. One as loving and happy as her grandparents had been. Fortunately, Mama had agreed to give her time. She hadn't wanted her daughter to make the same mistake she had. It wasn't Mama's fault Veronica had made the wrong decision, after all.

Veronica had been a woman of two and twenty when she'd finally taken a husband. If only she'd known then she was making the biggest mistake of her life. She shook her head. There was no point in mentally rehashing the past. Instead, she concentrated on her mother's solemn face. Poor, dear Mama had traveled from Whitmore Manor in Kent all the way to Essex to deliver this news to her daughter in person. That's how Veronica knew it was serious. More serious than all the other times Grandpapa had suffered a setback with his health. The man was six and eighty years of age. He'd endured an attack of the heart many months ago. The entire family had been worried about him since. After all, he couldn't live forever. No matter how much they wished for it. But it was especially awful to know that if he lived one more sennight, it would be his last holiday. His last Christmastide at Whitmore Manor.

Veronica clenched her jaw to fight the tears that had gathered at the back of her eyes. If Mama wasn't crying,

Veronica wouldn't start. It would only make Mama sadder. No, Veronica would be strong and show no emotion. She'd had enough practice over the last two years.

"How are Elizabeth and Jessica taking the news?" Veronica finally managed to ask. Her younger twin sisters still lived with Mama.

Mama inclined her head. "Elizabeth is stoic. Jessica is full of dramatics. As usual."

The hint of a smile glanced over Veronica's lips. That sounded right. Their looks may have been identical, but the twins' dispositions were the exact opposite of each other. They had turned eighteen in October and were preparing for their debuts in the spring. Elizabeth dreaded her come-out like a particularly noxious form of the plague, while Jessica waited on tenterhooks, barely able to contain her excitement.

"And Grandmama?" Veronica ventured, not looking forward to hearing how her darling eighty-year-old grandmother was handling the news that her husband of over six decades might pass away at any moment.

"As well as can be expected," Mama replied with a deep sigh.

Veronica expelled a long breath and placed her hands on her lap, staring at them numbly. "I shall return to Whitmore Manor with you tomorrow and ensure Grandpapa has the best, most comfortable holiday possible." She attempted a brave, hopeful smile, but wasn't at all certain the strained look that was surely on her face inspired any sort of confidence.

"I'm not going back to Whitmore Manor," Mama informed her, sitting up even straighter. "Not directly at least."

Veronica cocked her head to the side and frowned. "What? Where are you going?"

"I'm going to London tomorrow morning…to fetch Justin," Mama replied.

Veronica's frown deepened. Justin, her older brother, the marquess, was a bachelor and a profligate who spent most of his days in his London town house sleeping 'til noon, and his nights raking hell in a wide variety of the city's clubs and gambling establishments. Veronica hadn't spoken more than a handful of words to him in…two years. For excellent reason.

"Ah, yes, must fetch Justin," Veronica replied, a curt tone in her voice.

"Your brother has every right to know how ill your grandfather is," Mama replied evenly.

"You're right," Veronica allowed, feeling churlish. Mama knew precisely why her son and eldest daughter weren't on good terms. But Veronica and her brother faked niceties during family holidays for Grandpapa's sake. It would be no different this Christmastide. "Very well, Mama. Mary and I will set out for Whitmore Manor tomorrow. I will meet you there when you return from London with Justin."

Mama nodded before clearing her throat. She folded her gloved hands primly in her lap and met Veronica's gaze directly. "I traveled here to deliver the news in person for another reason also, my dear."

Veronica swallowed. Hard. Ever since Mama had entered the drawing room and been served a cup of tea, Veronica had been dreading this next part. The *real* reason for Mama's visit. Veronica had an awful feeling she knew just what it would be. She stared at her pretty mother with the dark hair and eyes that all four of her children had inherited. Mother's hair was streaked with gray now, but she was still quite beautiful. Veronica looked like her. Everyone said so. She only wished she were as gracious as Mama. And as strong.

Besides her grace, strength, and beauty, Mama was also

still a commanding presence when she chose to be, and she obviously chose to be at present. Her gaze never faltered. "Your grandfather has a final wish," Mama said, her serious tone conveying the importance of the pronouncement.

Veronica kept her face blank, but her insides had already dissolved into a roiling mass of nerves. She pressed her lips together tightly and delivered the barest hint of a nod.

"He wants the *entire* family together for Christmastide next week," Mama continued. "He wants to see *everyone*...a jovial group...one last time."

Veronica stiffened and forced herself to breathe normally. "I promise to be civil to Justin for the entire Christmastide holiday, if that's what you're worried about." But she already knew that *wasn't* what Mama was worried about...or what she was asking. Veronica's throat went dry just thinking about it. Nausea roiled in her gut.

"I'm not speaking of Justin," Mama replied, lifting her chin and giving her daughter the arched-brow stare Veronica hadn't seen since she was a girl and had sneaked out of the house to swim in the pond at Whitmore Manor in the middle of the night.

Veronica's nostrils flared. She lifted her chin, too. There was no use pretending any longer. "What if he refuses?" she reasoned, plucking absently at her dark-green skirts.

Mama's arched-brow stare remained firmly in place. "He may be a scoundrel, darling, but he's not a complete *beast*. How can he refuse the request of a dying man?"

It was on the tip of Veronica's tongue to ask Mama if *she* would ask him. Mama was already on her way to London to ask Justin the same question. She could easily stop by Edgefield's town house and ask him as well. After all, he wouldn't deny his *mother-in-law*, would he?

Veronica immediately frowned. Probably. She wasn't convinced that he wasn't a beast. But even if she had the nerve to ask Mama to intervene, Veronica knew she wouldn't do it. She couldn't do it. No. She would have to deal with *him* on her own. He was her problem. Not Mama's.

"Very well," Veronica said, with a sigh. "I'll be there."

"And?" Mama prodded, allowing her dark brow to drop back into place over her intensely dark eye.

Veronica shook her head in as nonchalant a manner as she dared and purposely didn't meet Mama's gaze. "And I'll do my best to get *him* to come as well," she promised, having absolutely no clue how she would accomplish such a feat.

"It's *not* a request, darling," Mama said in the voice that Veronica had only heard a few times in her life. One that clearly indicated her mother expected complete obedience.

"If he refuses, I cannot very well abduct him and bring him to Whitmore Manor in shackles." Frustration tinged Veronica's voice.

"I don't particularly care *how* you get him there," Mama replied with the hint of a smile before deftly lifting the teacup and taking a small, polite sip. She set the cup aside and stood. "Now, I'm off to rest before dinner."

Pressing her hand to her ribs, Veronica watched her mother go. Trepidation and nausea congealed in Veronica's middle. She'd been dreading a moment like this for two years. The two years it had been since she'd told her husband to go to hell, since she'd packed her belongings and left their London town house. Since she'd made it clear she intended to go to their country estate and expected him to give her fair warning before he ever came to the property, so she'd have ample time to vacate. In the entire two years, she'd never once received a letter from him, he'd never once come to visit, and she'd neither seen nor heard from him. Precisely how she preferred it.

But Grandpapa had always adored that arse, Edgefield. Her grandfather called him a young scalawag. Grandfather always saw the best in people. He'd been blinded by Sebastian's charm, had liked him since he was a child, coming to visit Justin on breaks from Eton. The two boys had been thick as thieves their whole lives...one of the many reasons that when it had come time to marry, Veronica had looked no further than her own older brother's best friend, Sebastian Sinclair, the Duke of Edgefield.

He'd fooled everyone, not just Grandpapa. In fact, she'd been the biggest fool of all.

But Grandpapa was special to her, and he was dying. She'd always been his favorite. The entire family knew it. When she was a little girl, he'd sneaked her favorite lemon cakes from the grand balls thrown at Whitmore Manor. He'd taken her driving in his curricle, allowing her to hold the reins as soon as they were out of Mama's eyesight. He'd taught her how to shoot a rifle and had been her first partner when she learned the waltz. Her entire life, Grandpapa had always been there for her with a bit of wit and wisdom when she'd been feeling down or needed a shoulder to lean on. She loved him immeasurably. Yes. Veronica would do *anything* for her beloved grandfather...even ask her awful, cheating husband to come to one last Christmastide house party and *pretend* to be happy.

Veronica stood and stared out the windows across the meadow behind the estate. An enormous oak tree stood tall and proud, not far from the window, its branches stark against the gray winter sky. When she and Sebastian had first married and he'd brought her here, it had been summer. The tree had been full of lush leaves, and she'd loved the unobstructed view of it from this room. She'd pictured them there...herself, Sebastian, and children...four of them. The same number Mama had. All with dark hair like both of their parents. Though hopefully at least one would inherit his father's unforgettable green eyes. She had seen them all there, in her mind's eye, under the shade of the grand tree, talking and laughing, laying on a soft quilt, warmed by the sun, watching the clouds peeking through the branches. *A happy family.* All she'd ever wanted. Now, given the circumstances, there was little chance she would ever be a mother.

Veronica swallowed the lump that had formed in her throat. The memory was painful. She wanted to erase it from her mind. And yet...she still insisted on taking callers in this room and she never asked for the curtains to be drawn. Clearly, she was a glutton for punishment.

She took a deep breath to clear her head of impossible fantasies, then she turned swiftly toward the door and marched from the room. She would ask Mary, her maid, to pack her trunk immediately. Veronica would leave for London tomorrow as well. But her mission differed from her mother's. Veronica was going to town to convince the man she never wanted to see again to come to Christmastide at Whitmore Manor and pretend to be half of a loving, happy couple for the better part of a sennight. The thought sickened her. And the next thought sickened her even more. How in the world would she get him to agree to it?

# CHAPTER TWO

*London, The Duke of Edgefield's Town House, the next evening*

Sebastian Sinclair, The Duke of Edgefield, stomped up the curving marble staircase and into his bedchamber. He ripped off his cravat and tossed the thing on the sapphire blue satin coverlet that enveloped his bed. "Chadwick," he called, already impatient that his valet wasn't waiting for him.

The door to his wardrobe flew open and Chadwick came hurrying out of the smaller adjoining room. "Your Grace," Chadwick said, bowing. "Forgive me. I didn't know precisely when you'd return. I—"

"Come help me off with this coat. I must be at the Markhams' affair within the hour. The bloody Parliamentary session ran long at Westminster tonight."

"Of course, Your Grace." The man sprinted forth and began helping Sebastian remove his coat, while Sebastian made quick work of the buttons on his shirt.

Sebastian frowned to himself. He shouldn't have been so curt and demanding of Chadwick. Sebastian had been in the devil's own mood lately—oh, who was he kidding? He'd been in the devil's own mood for over two years now—but he shouldn't take it out on the hapless valet.

Sebastian allowed the man to pull off his coat, then he took a seat on the padded bench in front of the bed while Chadwick kneeled before him to remove his boots.

"I'll wear the black tonight," Sebastian said offhandedly. "Is my bath prepared?"

"Yes, Your Grace," Chadwick hastened to assure him.

After his boots and stockings had been removed, Sebastian dismissed the man. Then he pulled off his breeches and tossed them atop the bed. Naked, he stalked across the room toward the smaller room opposite his wardrobe. He purposely avoided looking at the east door that led from his bedchamber. That was the one that led to...*her* room. Antipathy coiled in his belly. He couldn't stand to even think of her name.

The moment Sebastian pushed open the door to the bathing chamber, his tight shoulders relaxed. Steam filled the room, and across the space, a full tub awaited him. Next to the copper tub was a small wooden table where a fluffy towel, a bar of soap in a small dish, and a straight razor sat. Normally, he'd ask Chadwick to shave him, but it was more efficient this way.

Sebastian had sent a note ahead asking the valet to leave out the razor along with the other items for his bath. He must make haste. The Christmastide season was always full of commitments, including dinner parties, holiday gatherings, and many other sorts of affairs Sebastian was obligated to attend. Most of them put him on edge. The Markhams' event would be no different. Lord Markham would no doubt ask for his vote for the upcoming Reform bill in Parliament, a subject Sebastian was more than tired of discussing. He'd made his thoughts quite clear on the subject. He was a Whig and would vote with the Whigs. Markham refused to take his answer as final.

But the parties and the bill weren't what truly had Sebastian in the devil's own mood tonight. He could handle those insignificant bothers deftly enough. No. Tonight he was in a rotten temper because Lord Hazelton—that unmitigated arse —had had the temerity to ask Sebastian about his *wife*. His least favorite subject.

"How *is* the duchess?" Hazelton had drawled in a fake-innocent voice as if he hadn't the faintest clue what a sore subject *the duchess* was for Sebastian. "Seems as if Society has been missing her for a bit. She's not *ill* again, is she?"

It was longer than 'a bit' and they both bloody well knew it. It had been two years. Two years and three months, to be precise, but who was keeping count? Regardless, it would be a frigid day in Hades before Sebastian let a fool like Hazelton see that he'd been affected by his words.

"She's well," Sebastian had answered smoothly. Clearly, he'd used the excuse that Veronica was ill one too many times. "I'll have to speak with my lady about gracing London's ballrooms more often."

Hazelton knew it was a damn lie. The entire *ton* knew Veronica had left Sebastian. Or at least the rumor mill had been correct when it reported that she'd packed her trunks only two months after their enormous July wedding and left for their country estate in Essex. Noticeably *without* her husband, with whom she'd appeared to be so in love only days prior.

No one had seen her since. Least of all, Sebastian. But he had it on good authority from his closest friend and Veronica's brother, Justin Whitmoreland, that she was, in fact, alive and well, if still nursing a huge grudge against her husband. A grudge Sebastian wholeheartedly returned. But he'd be damned before he admitted to the *ton* that at the age of eight and twenty, he'd been left by his wife. Instead, he'd done what any good nobleman would do under the same circumstances and acted as if nothing was amiss. Her Grace merely preferred the countryside as far as Sebastian was concerned, and he needn't explain that to a bloody soul. How he would explain that he hadn't produced an heir and never would, was a different matter entirely, and one that he refused to dwell on for long. Whenever the disturbing thought arrived on the doorstep of his mind, he ignored it completely, preferring instead to toss himself into his work, his boxing matches, or Parliamentary proceedings. Anything to take his mind off the fact that not only had he failed as a husband, but he also would never be a father.

Justin helped a great deal in perpetuating the illness story, and between the two of them they'd managed to, if not convince anyone that Her Grace was in the countryside for reasons other than an unhappy marriage, at least generate enough doubt that no one had asked Sebastian directly for the truth...until Hazelton's little venture today.

And of course that arse hadn't left it at that. "Excellent," Hazelton had replied. "So, Her Grace *will be* at our Twelfth Night ball next month? She's missed the last two, I seem to recall."

The statement had been followed by a sly smile, one Sebastian had wanted to knock off Hazelton's face with his fist. *That* was the reason Sebastian had lost his damn mind and instead of making some excuse, had said, "We'll be there," before stalking past Hazelton, a muscle ticking in his jaw.

The entire ride home, Sebastian had slapped his leather gloves against his thigh, damning himself for a fool for allowing Hazelton to get to him. Of course *they* wouldn't be there. His duchess wouldn't even speak to him, let alone attend a ball with him and pretend to be happy. Damn. Damn. Damn. He'd eventually have to make his excuses to

Hazelton. He couldn't say she was ill *again*, could he? No. He'd need to invent a new excuse this time.

He ground his teeth as he lowered himself into the bath. Two years was a long time for a wife to hide in the countryside. Perhaps he'd finally be forced to write to that shrew he'd married and tell her he'd be coming for a visit. That would prompt her to vacate the countryside. She had to be getting bored out there all alone in that giant house. Still, it didn't guarantee she'd come to London, and it certainly didn't mean she'd attend any events with him.

Hazelton wasn't the only one talking, however. That fool was simply the only one who had the impudence to confront Sebastian. He'd heard the rumors. London was abuzz, wondering at the long absence of the Duchess of Edgefield. The unlovable duke. That's what they were calling him. Would he eventually be forced to admit his wife had left him? That perhaps she'd never even loved him. Just like his mother.

These were the thoughts that rambled through Sebastian's mind as he began soaping himself up. He nearly growled as he dunked the soap into the hot water and lathered himself thoroughly.

Christmas Day was next week. Once again, he'd be alone for the blasted holiday. Well, not alone precisely, but not with any semblance of a proper family either. He couldn't even spend Christmastide at his closest friend's house in the country because that family included *her*. That irked him even more. Before he'd married Veronica, his family had been...Veronica's family. Or Justin's at least, which, of course, was the same family. Sebastian had *thought* he'd married the girl next door, instead he'd married a woman who believed the worst of him. Just like his mother. Damn it. He'd never been so wrong about something in his life.

He'd spent Christmastide with Justin's family for years

after his own father had died. The viper who'd given birth to him had long ago stopped even pretending to want to spend the holiday with him. She spent the Season in Bath with friends. But for the last two years, unable to spend the holiday with the Whitmorelands, Sebastian had been forced to call upon his next closest friend, Selby. And while Selby was a loyal friend and a fine chap, his family just wasn't the same as the Whitmorelands. They didn't joke with each other, or play games competitively, or open their gifts the morning of Christmas Eve for no other reason besides blatant impatience. No. The Selbys weren't the Whitmorelands, and they never would be.

Regardless, Sebastian would spend the blasted week at Selby's, trying to fight off his friend's overly affectionate— and often inebriated—Aunt Minnie and having to speak in an overly loud voice to Selby's Uncle Teddy, who was significantly hard of hearing.

A sharp rap at the door to the bath chamber pulled Sebastian from his thoughts. "Yes," he called, more than a little peeved that his bath was being interrupted.

Hawthorne, his butler, pushed open the door and strode inside. The man stood at attention, staring directly at the marble wall in front of him.

"Yes, Hawthorne," Sebastian shot out. "What is so bloody important that it couldn't wait until I'm dressed?"

Hawthorne's blue eyes remained trained on the wall, but his jaw flinched. "It's Her Grace," he said in a voice that sounded like a man who sorely regretted having to proclaim this information. "She's in the silver drawing room and she demands to speak with you immediately."

If a small dragon had flown into the bathing chamber and dropped a bar of soap directly in front of his face, causing a splash, Sebastian couldn't have been more surprised. "*Her Grace?*" he asked, narrowing his eyes and drawing out the words into a long, confused question, more trying to reconcile the thought in his brain than truly asking the man to repeat himself.

"Her Grace," Hawthorne repeated, painfully. "The Duchess of Edgefield."

"My *wife*?" Sebastian clarified, his eyes still narrowed. All the words were English, yet they still made little sense.

"Yes, Your Grace," Hawthorne answered. "And I wouldn't have bothered you under such conditions, however, she…" the poor man trailed off, clearing his throat uncomfortably.

Sebastian arched a brow. "She insisted, did she, Hawthorne?"

"Quite emphatically, Your Grace," Hawthorne replied with a definite nod.

"It's all right, Hawthorne." Sebastian rubbed his chin between his thumb and forefinger. "I know *precisely* how demanding she can be."

The butler's only reply was another blank-faced nod.

Sebastian continued soaping his arms and chest. Hmm. This was interesting. Veronica was here. He hadn't spoken to the woman in over two years, and she was here, demanding he speak to her. Which could only mean one thing…she *wanted* something from him. *That* was interesting.

But he wasn't about to snap to her merest demand. She could bloody well *wait*.

He soaped his hair and dunked himself beneath the hot, bubbly water before slowly reaching for the razor. By God, he was bathing, and he wouldn't rush just because *she* had arrived on his doorstep demanding he speak to her. But he had to tell Hawthorne something. The poor man was wilting in the steamy heat of the chamber.

"Tell *Her Grace* I'm indisposed at the moment and will be down within the hour," Sebastian finally offered.

"Yes, Your Grace," Hawthorne replied, bowing, turning,

and hurrying from the room.

Sebastian spent the next several minutes doing his best to shave his shadow of a beard with the razor, using his fingertips to gauge where he needed to stroke. He'd been in something of a hurry before, but now he took his time, quite pleased with the thought of making *her* wait.

He was nearly finished shaving when another knock sounded on the door. "Come in," he called, more than a bit disgruntled at having been interrupted again.

The door opened slowly, and Hawthorne stepped inside. As before, the butler had a stoic look on his face and kept his eyes trained on the far wall. "Your Grace," he began. "I regret to inform you that Her Grace has demanded that you come down from whatever indisposition you're—*ahem*—entertaining and meet with her immediately."

"She said that?" Sebastian shot out, his nostrils flaring and eyes narrowing.

"Yes," Hawthorne replied, looking as if he'd rather be anywhere else. "Her exact words were, 'Tell him I've no intention of waiting while he sneaks his latest mistress down the back staircase.'"

Sebastian clenched his jaw until a muscle ticked in his cheek. That sounded exactly like her, quick to assume and quicker to judge. Wouldn't she be horrified to know he'd merely been in his bath when—

Wait a moment. Sebastian stopped, poking out his cheek with his tongue. If she was going to be demanding, he would give her *precisely* what she wanted. "Fine," he snapped. "Escort her up."

"Your Grace?" The servant's eyes flared with what appeared to be panic. "Here?"

"You heard me, Hawthorne." A calculating smile curled Sebastian's lips. "Escort my wife up here, directly. I look forward to her visit."

# CHAPTER THREE

Veronica followed Hawthorne up the sweeping marble staircase that led to the second floor of Sebastian's opulent town house. The poor servant had come back down and informed her in a voice that could only be described as distressed, "His Grace has indicated that if you're not inclined to wait, you may come up to his bedchamber."

Veronica had fought the urge to allow her jaw to drop. Instead, she'd narrowed her eyes and contemplated the matter. What was Sebastian up to? She had expected little from him, but he was clearly attempting to call her bluff. And she wasn't about to let him get away with it. If he wanted to embarrass himself and his mistress by inviting his *wife* to enter the room, she would surprise them both. After all, Veronica had long ago stopped being hurt by the notion that he shared his bed with another woman. Mostly. Although she'd never actually *witnessed* it before. This would be a first.

Regardless, she refused to allow Sebastian to get the upper hand, and she did not intend to cool her heels in the drawing room any longer, waiting for his exalted presence. She hadn't been able to leave for London until much later than she'd hoped this morning. As a result, it was nearly nine o'clock, and it had been a long day. She wanted this over as quickly as possible. She would march directly upstairs and say what she had to say.

"This way," came Hawthorne's tortured voice as they reached the top of the stairs and he turned to the right.

"Yes, I remember," she said, before biting her lip. She hadn't meant to be rude to the unfortunate servant. It wasn't his fault his master was a horse's arse.

"Of course, Your Grace," he replied. If Hawthorne—the epitome of skill and polish—was turning red, she would never mention it. She regretted he was forced to be in the middle of this unfortunate little *scene*.

When they arrived at the bedchamber door, Hawthorne knocked, while Veronica experienced an unexpected moment of dread. Had she been wrong to come here? Had she been wrong to taunt Sebastian? Had she been wrong to insist he see her immediately? It was one thing to be perturbed in the drawing room, but it was quite another to be standing in front of the man's bedchamber door—a bedchamber in which they'd had *many* nights of *unforgettable* lovemaking—about to see him tangled in the sheets with his light-o'-love. Terror clutched at her middle.

Veronica nearly turned and scurried back down to the drawing room. But that would give Sebastian the upper hand in the negotiations that were soon to follow, and she would die before she did that. No. Whatever she was about to witness behind that closed door was her own blasted fault. She swallowed and forced herself to lift her chin. Besides, he should be the one embarrassed by his behavior. She had done nothing wrong.

"Come in," came a voice she would never forget. Deep and authoritative, with a hint of arrogance and a trace of humor. It still sent an unwanted tingle down her spine. She blew out a deep breath. She'd had hours in the coach today to prepare for this moment...but somehow, she still wasn't prepared. She wiped her sweaty gloved palms on the violet pelisse she'd refused to remove downstairs. She hadn't intended to stay long enough.

Hawthorne pushed open the door and stepped inside while Veronica waited behind the servant. She set her blurred focus on a painting of a hunting scene on the far side of the room while the butler said, "Her Grace, the Duchess of Edgefield, to see you, Your Grace."

Then she took a step. First one, then another, until she was standing fully inside Sebastian's bedchamber for the first time in over two years. The familiar scent of his soap, the same scent she'd licked off his sweaty neck on more than one occasion, nearly sent her to her knees. She clenched her jaw and forced herself to swing her gaze to the side...to look at him. Whatever there was to see, she might as well get it over with.

She frowned. He wasn't in bed. Her eyes scanned the wide mattress with the familiar dark-blue coverlet. It was not only empty but entirely made as if it hadn't been used at all in the last, say, hour. Her gaze continued around the room until it alighted on him.

And *that's* when her jaw dropped. She couldn't help it this time.

Standing near the wardrobe, a fire crackling in the large hearth behind him, was her estranged husband. And the man was wearing nothing more than a white towel slung low around his hips. She allowed her gaze to travel from his bare feet, up his strong calves, to his thighs outlined by the towel, then along his muscled abdomen, to his chiseled chest and wide shoulders. She swallowed. Hard. Oh, this had been a bad idea. She shouldn't have come up here. Still, she couldn't force her gaze away.

Instead, she continued her perusal. His dark hair was wet and an unmistakable smirk—one she also knew too well—rode his handsome, firmly molded lips. His eyes glowed like emeralds beneath his unfairly long black lashes.

"You may go, Hawthorne," Sebastian said, pulling a fresh white cravat from the wardrobe in front of him.

Hawthorne removed himself from the room so quickly Veronica was convinced she'd felt a breeze from the tails of his livery coat.

Sebastian turned away from her and she swallowed again while her eyes moved up from his legs covered with a dusting of dark hair, over his arse, which was *fine* even when hidden by a towel, to his muscled back and shoulders still teaming with droplets of water from his bath.

She cleared her throat to ensure her voice was still there. "Where is she?" she asked in a tone that she could only hope was both nonchalant and uninterested.

"Who?" he replied simply, as he continued to pull clothing items from the wardrobe.

That cursed towel looked as if it might drop from his hips at any moment and, for the life of her, she couldn't decide if that would be a *bad* thing. Very well. Yes. Bad. *Quite* bad.

"You know quite well who…Melissa." Veronica could barely push the hated name past her lips. She prayed she still sounded unaffected.

He turned then, and his green gaze met hers. A grin covered his face, and he shrugged. "I've no idea where she is," he said simply. "In fact, your guess is as good as mine."

Veronica crossed her arms over her chest and eyed him warily. "No doubt she's still in the bath," she said, nodding toward the bath chamber, desperately hoping her voice continued to sound blasé rather than angry or jealous.

Because she was *not* jealous. She was not and she never would be. It was a fool's lot to be jealous over a man who could not be faithful. If she'd learned nothing else, it was that.

"You're welcome to look," he offered, nodding toward the bath chamber as he used another towel to dry off his considerably muscled chest.

She hadn't seen the man in two years, and he'd certainly been muscled back then, but he was more muscled now. His biceps bulging, his pectorals swelling, his abdomen outlined in six clearly defined packs. Her mouth went dry. She was looking all right. But not at what he'd offered.

She forced herself to swing her gaze toward the bath chamber door. She *wanted* to go look. Drat it. She was *sorely tempted* to go look. But that would imply that she cared, and she would rather be dead than allow him to think *that* for one moment. "No matter," she said, still trying to sound completely unaffected.

"I haven't seen Melissa since the night that you—"

"Please." Veronica put up a violet-gloved hand and glanced away, completely unable to hear another word on the subject. They'd had this discussion…at length. More than once. And the fact remained that he was a liar and a cheater, and no amount of discussion would change that.

"Fine." He placed his hands on his nearly bare hips. "Why are you here, Veronica?"

Hearing her name on his lips did something to her. It brought back a memory of him whispering it in her ear when he was so deep inside her that—No. Her breath came out in a heated rush. That sort of thinking was not helping. She swallowed and tugged at the top button of her brocade-covered pelisse, which was currently choking her in the ungodly hot room. Where was a fan when one needed one? "I've come because…" She swallowed again, but for an

21

entirely different reason this time. "My grandfather is dying."

Sebastian's chin jerked up momentarily. "I'm sorry to hear that," he said with a genuine warmth that nearly made tears spring to Veronica's eyes.

She shook her head to rid herself of the unwanted emotion, reminding herself of her mission. "He's gravely ill and Mama says..." She bit her lip, unable to say the words out loud now that the time had come, even though she'd practiced them in the carriage over and over.

"He's unlikely to live much longer?" Sebastian prompted in a solemn tone.

She didn't want to feel grateful that he'd saved her from having to say the awful, the obvious. But she was. She nodded. "Yes."

"And?" he prompted.

She couldn't concentrate while he was wearing a towel, for heaven's sake. She shook herself and averted her gaze. "And...I thought you should know," she finished. Blast. Why couldn't she just come out and say what she must? She dared a glance at him again.

He scrubbed a hand through the back of his wet hair and narrowed his eyes on her. "Look, I know you're here for a reason, and that reason isn't merely to tell me your grandfather is ill. Justin could have told me that. What do you want?"

Blast again. She was making a mess of this. She pressed her lips together tightly and sucked air into her nostrils. It was time. And if she didn't word this correctly, Sebastian might refuse. Her grandfather's happiness in his last days depended on this. She swallowed again and said the words as evenly as she could while bile rose in her throat. "I want you to come to Christmastide at Whitmore Manor...with me."

His dark brows shot up, but the look of surprise was

quickly replaced with one of suspicion. "Wait." He cocked his head to the side and eyed her warily. "*Why?*"

Arms still folded, she impatiently drummed her fingers against her elbows and gave an impatient sigh. "Justin hasn't told you?"

"Told me what?" Sebastian asked, eyes still narrowed.

She straightened her shoulders and shifted uncomfortably on her booted feet. "That we've never told Grandfather that we...that you and I are..." Her voice trailed off. She wanted to kick herself for being unable to complete the sentence.

Only one of Sebastian's eyebrows arched this time. "That you accused me of being unfaithful and refuse to listen to the truth?"

She spun on her heel, reaching for the door handle. "I've no intention of rehashing this tired subject again. If you only wish to argue, I'll leave. We've both said all we have to say on that matter, I believe."

"Wait."

She froze. Still facing away from him, she closed her eyes briefly and thanked the heavens he'd stopped her because she didn't know how she'd get him to agree to come with her if she left now. She shouldn't have threatened to leave. But she hadn't been able to countenance arguing with him again about *Melissa*.

Letting her hand fall from the door handle, Veronica turned slowly back toward him. Her features were carefully blank.

Sebastian had an equally inscrutable look on his face. "I agree," he replied, in an even tone. "We *have* said all that needs saying to each other. But tell me, why haven't you told your grandfather...about us?"

Veronica turned her face to the side, trying not to remember the night they'd had mind-numbing sex on the chair just to her right, and the fact that even now—even when she couldn't stand the sight of him—she wanted to do it again. She couldn't help her body's response to seeing him half nude. She was only human, after all. The man was… regrettably…*gorgeous.*

She cleared her throat and kept her gaze averted. "His health has been poor. Mama thought it best if we…didn't burden Grandfather with such…unhappy news." There. That was true.

"So, your grandfather does not know we've been estranged?" Sebastian shook his head, a humorless smile quirking up the side of his lips.

"That is correct." She couldn't help herself. She let her glance slide over his body again and plucked at the neck of her pelisse. *Why* was it so infernally hot in here? She forced herself to look away once more.

"That's why you're here?" Sebastian said, clearly piecing together her entire predicament as a wide grin spread across his lips. "You want me to come to Christmastide at Whitmore Manor and *pretend* that we are still in love."

"No." The word shot from her mouth like a ball from a pistol. He'd guessed correctly, of course, but his words had slashed across her heart. One word in particular: 'still.' He was taunting her. *She* had been in love with *him*, madly so, but he…he had *never* loved her. He'd merely used her as a means to an end, a titled lady with good manners from an impeccable family to take as a wife and bear his heirs. He had never let his emotions into their marriage. He'd never intended to. But she would die before she gave him the satisfaction. And she *refused* to allow him to pretend he had loved her back.

But her response had been far too quick. She needed to regain control of the conversation. She straightened her shoulders and forced a half-hearted smile to her lips. "I want you to come with me to Christmastide at Whitmore Manor and pretend that we are happily married," she clarified.

He eyed her carefully, clearly still suspicious. "Why?"

She paused. She had to choose her next words carefully. "It's…Grandfather…" She cleared her throat and began again. "Mama thought it would be nice if we all spend Christmastide together. One la…last Christmastide." She couldn't keep her voice from faltering.

"Your *mother*, you say?" Sebastian narrowed his eyes on Veronica and rubbed his freshly shaved chin.

"Y…yes," she insisted, biting her lip.

"It's not your *grandfather's* wish, then?" He paused for a moment, still eyeing her carefully. "His *dying* wish?"

In her mind, Veronica let fly a string of expletives. Outwardly, however, she merely pressed her lips together and blinked, struggling to keep her face entirely blank. Why did Sebastian have to be so clever? Shouldn't a man gifted with his good looks stand to be a bit dull in the mind? It was unfair. She remained silent, contemplating her next statement. It would only hurt her case that he'd realized it was Grandpapa's dying wish. Sebastian knew how much she loved her grandfather.

Apparently, her silence was all the affirmation Sebastian needed, however. "I'm correct, am I not?" he asked, his grin widening, making her want to stalk across the rug and slap it off his handsome face.

"Grandpapa has always adored Christmastide," she said. There. That was all she intended to allow him.

The infuriating grin remained. "I see. So, the question is…" Sebastian tugged at the towel on his hips and her eyes were inexorably drawn to the line of hair that trailed down his flat belly and disappeared beneath the towel. She immediately averted her gaze to the fine rug below her black leather traveling boots. This was torture, plain and simple.

25

"Wh…what's the question?" she asked, forcing herself to remember why she was here. And it was certainly not to ogle the man. She did, however, glance back at him.

His eyes narrowed, and he caught his plump lower lip between two white teeth. "The question is…what are you willing to do in return for my…compliance?"

She lifted her chin and met his green gaze. This was it. The moment of truth. Expelling her breath, she asked, "What do you want in return?" Her voice was higher than she intended, a bit more tremulous than she would have liked, but at least they'd finally got to the place she'd been dreading since Mama had arrived on her doorstep yesterday afternoon. It was time for Sebastian to name his terms.

He poked his tongue into his cheek, crossed his arms over his bare chest, and lifted one dark eyebrow like the complete rogue that he was. "Seems to me that compliance for compliance is a fair trade."

Her heart hammering in her chest, she bit the inside of her cheek to keep from saying something she ought not. "What sort of compliance?" She forced the words past her dry lips.

He cocked his head to the side, a boyish smile on his lips. "I will come with you, and I will play the part of the doting husband in every way…on two conditions."

"Which are?" The words shot from her throat, and she nearly choked on them. Her hands shook, and she crossed her arms over her middle and tucked them beneath her elbows to keep him from noticing. *Two* conditions? She fought the urge to roll her eyes. Of course there would be two. Not just one. Though she supposed she ought to be happy he hadn't said three.

He nodded efficiently. "First, after Christmastide at Whitmore Manor, you must return here, to London, and attend the Hazeltons' Twelfth Night ball with me. Also pretending that we are not estranged."

"Done," she said so quickly his eyebrow quirked again. That wasn't so bad. Attending the Hazeltons' ball would be a small price to pay for Grandpapa's happiness. "What is the second condition?" she asked hastily.

When a slow, triumphant smile spread across his lips, revealing his perfectly straight teeth, she knew the second condition would be much less simple to grant.

He moved toward her, stopping mere steps away, and she could smell the scent of his cologne. The same cologne that used to make her weak in the knees. Blast it. The same cologne that apparently *still* made her weak in the knees because she had to brace a hand on the chest of drawers that sat next to the doorway to prepare herself for his next words.

His eyes bore into her. "You cannot be ignorant of the fact that our, ahem, estrangement has prevented me from doing my duty. I need an heir."

The room spun. Veronica's breath came in small pants. Her chest ached. Her nipples turned to hard buds. "What are you saying, Sebastian?" But she already knew. She already knew *exactly* what he was about to say. And God help her, she *wanted* him to say it. Craved it, actually.

"In addition to the Twelfth Night ball, I will travel with you and play the part of the doting husband in exchange for your willing participation the entire time…" He paused, and his smoldering gaze captured hers once more. "*In bed.*"

# CHAPTER FOUR

Three days later, Sebastian sat across from Veronica in his well-appointed traveling coach as they made their way from Edgefield Hall toward Whitmore Manor. The journey would take the better part of the day, even with Sebastian's finest horses at the start. Their coach and the second one carrying the servants would arrive at Whitmore Manor in the late afternoon.

Veronica had agreed to Sebastian's second condition in London with much less resistance than he'd expected. Her face had flushed, and she'd been uncharacteristically silent for several moments, but she'd finally jerked her head in a decisive nod and said, "Very well. I agree to your terms," as if they'd just set out a marriage contract giving her rights to an allowance and not agreed to spend the next fortnight together wrapped in bedsheets. Perhaps he should have asked for her attendance at *two* balls when they returned to London. He smiled to himself. Probably best not to press his good fortune.

The entire arrangement still surprised Sebastian. He'd merely been trying to provoke her when he'd asked to share her bed. He'd expected her to balk at his outlandish request. She did *so* like to argue. Frankly, the request had flown from his lips before he'd had much of a chance to consider it. Of course, he needed an heir, but the way he'd nearly leered at her when he'd requested her participation in bed was bad form. He blamed her nearness, the alluring lily scent of her perfume, and the fact that he hadn't had a woman in over two years. But instead of balking, she'd agreed rather readily. And he couldn't quite bring himself to regret his request.

After accepting his terms, Veronica had insisted on spending the night at her brother's town house. Apparently, her mother was there as well. Then Veronica had hurried back to Essex. Sebastian had promised to fetch her this morning and escort her to Kent so they would arrive to the holiday celebration together, a sign of solidarity and their first pretense of being a happily wedded pair. So far, however, the ride had been anything *but* happy. They were nearly at Whitmore Manor, and they'd barely said a handful of words to each other. Veronica had kept her nose buried in ladies' fashion periodicals. A useless thing to do—as far as Sebastian was concerned—for a lady who refused to come to London and be seen in Society.

Meanwhile, Sebastian had been doing his damnedest to ignore...or more correctly, to *stop being distracted by* her. He'd brought along the ledgers from his solicitor in London and had spent the better part of the journey balancing the damn things on his lap while trying to read them. But he found his gaze drawn again and again to Veronica. She'd always been beautiful. Her looks were one of the many things that had attracted him to her, after all. But there was something else about her now. Something more sharp, more distinguished, that made it difficult for him to tear his gaze from her countenance.

Her fine cheekbones were set below obsidian eyes framed

by thick black lashes. She had dark brows and a piercing gaze. The fullest lips that made him want to… He shook his head. He'd nearly forgotten how lovely she was. But the moment she'd stepped inside his bedchamber three nights ago, he'd been reminded immediately. Even with her lustrous hair swept up and hidden beneath a fashionable hat, she'd affected him. He remembered only too well what it felt like to let the long strands filter through his fingers while he rode her, her gasps of pleasure filling the room, her fingernails raking down his back.

Damn. Sebastian shook his head again. Such thoughts were altogether unhelpful. There'd be time enough to think about such things after they were safely in their bedchamber together at Whitmore Manor. And they *would* share a bedchamber. He'd insisted upon it. Along with their original agreement.

Now, he was doing a bollocks job of ignoring her while she could have won a prize for acting as if *he* didn't exist. Not once had he caught her looking at him, all the many times he'd glanced her way.

"I seem to recall you being more adept at conversation," he finally said, in an effort to taunt her into speaking to him. He'd already learned that niceties and politeness got him nothing more than half-hearted, one-syllable replies.

Without taking her eyes from her periodical, she merely said, "I seem to recall you telling me you'd given up your mistress. Memories can be faulty."

Sebastian's nostrils flared. "I *did* give up my mistress."

"And went back to her weeks later," Veronica replied, a fake-sweet smile on her face. She still refused to look at him.

She was obviously trying to rile him, which he admittedly deserved for trying to rile her. But *her* attempt had worked, which bothered him. "I did *not* go back to her weeks later," he replied simply.

Veronica arched a brow but continued to stare at the reading material she'd lifted in front of her face to no doubt block her view of him. "Oh, so you *didn't* lie to me about going to the club and visit her instead?"

He cursed under his breath. "Yes, I did, but—" He stopped himself and pinched the bridge of his nose momentarily before shaking it off and replacing it with a forced grin. "Let's have a more productive conversation, shall we?"

Finally, she folded down the edge of her periodical and eyed him over the top of the blasted thing. "'Productive?'" Her voice dripped with skepticism. "Such as?"

"I propose we come up with the ground rules for our little…agreement," he offered, settling back into his seat and crossing his arms over his chest.

Her dark brows shot up. "'Agreement?' Is that what we're calling it?"

"You are free to change your mind any time you like," he pointed out, giving her a tight smile. "Merely say the word. I can turn the coach right around and take you back to Whitmore Manor. Besides, why should you be the only one to benefit from the situation?"

She rolled her eyes. "Because you're a gentleman?"

His brows shot up. "Am I? I thought I was a rogue and a cheat. Which is it?" Of course, he was only trying to rile her again. Even if she called off their intimate arrangement, he wouldn't desert her. Her grandfather had always been kind to him and welcomed him when he'd had only his awful mother to call family. Sebastian hated to know he was dying. The truth was that Sebastian looked forward to seeing the old man again, seeing all of them again. The Whitmorelands were the only genuine family he'd ever known.

Veronica lifted her pert nose in the air and narrowed her dark eyes on him. "You clearly *are* a rogue and a cheat, and your conditions merely confirm it."

31

He rolled *his* eyes this time. "It must be so simple to live in your black and white world, without nuance or subtlety to confuse things."

She slapped a palm atop the periodical and drummed her nails on it, glaring at him. "What is *that* supposed to mean?"

He folded his arms across his chest. "You tried and convicted me in your head for a crime I didn't commit."

She leaned toward him, her eyes flashing with stark anger. "Don't you dare attempt to make me feel insane. Did you or did you not *admit* to it?"

He tightened his arms and clenched his jaw. "I admitted to *lying* to you. I *never* admitted to cheating."

She glared at him. "Parsing words as usual. Lying to one's wife. *What* a charming trait. Regardless, as you said, let's change the subject. What are these rules you want to set?"

Shaking off his frustration, Sebastian forced himself to take a deep breath. His wife could drive him mad more quickly than anyone. In more ways than one. But arguing with her was pointless. "First, I believe we should set a limit on the rules."

Eyeing him warily, she nodded. "That seems reasonable. Let's say...three each?"

He nodded too. "Very well. Ladies first." He gave her a tight smile.

Veronica tapped her fingers against the top of the periodical again for a few moments before speaking. Her eyes flared with obvious enlightenment as she decided what she would say. "*My* first rule is that I don't have to pretend to like you when Grandpapa is not present."

Sebastian couldn't stop his bark of laugher. He shook his head. "Heaven forbid. Fine. Then *my* first rule is you don't have to pretend to like me, but you cannot be *rude* to me, or ignore me."

"Fine," she allowed. She leaned back against the emerald

velvet squabs, a smile on her face, clearly warming to the subject. "My *second* rule is no kissing...on the lips."

Sebastian frowned. "That's preposterous. I'm going to take you to *bed*. How can we not kiss?"

She shrugged and arched a brow again. "I don't know, and I don't care, but that's my rule." She glared at him, daring him to defy her stipulation.

His nostrils flared. Damn it. Perhaps he shouldn't have agreed to three rules. He was already regretting it. "*My* second rule is that *you* cannot have any *other* rules limiting what we do in bed...within reason, of course. Let's say... anything we've done before is fair game." He arched a brow, and met her gaze, daring her to recall the many times when he'd had her begging for more and gasping his name.

Pink exploded on her cheeks, and she jerked her head to the side to stare out the window. He could tell she was smoldering inside. "Fine, then I reserve my *third* rule for some time before the fortnight is out."

He eyed her carefully. What was she planning? It couldn't possibly be worse than 'no kissing,' could it? On second thought, he didn't want to know. But he'd already agreed to the idea of setting three rules each. He couldn't go back on his word. "Then I reserve the same," he said. At least he might counteract her last rule with one of his own.

"Fine," Veronica replied before settling back into her seat and burying her face in the periodical once more. She tugged up the fur on her lap, ostensibly to ward off the chill in the air.

Arms still firmly crossed over his chest, Sebastian turned his head and stared out the window at the barren December landscape. How in the hell had his once-promising marriage turned into this?

~

VERONICA WISTFULLY PERUSED the latest fashions. It was ridiculous to care about such things when she hadn't been in Society for so long, but she did so love beautiful clothing. Though she'd barely been able to concentrate on the periodical what with Sebastian sitting not a stone's throw away from her, the familiar scent of his cologne teasing her nostrils and reminding her of a half a score of memories she desperately wanted to erase from her mind.

Every rotation of the coach's wheels carried them closer and closer to Whitmore Manor...closer and closer to *their bedchamber* at Whitmore Manor. The thought made Veronica both anxious and (if she was being honest) excited. She agreed to Sebastian's outrageous condition for three reasons. First, she wasn't exactly in the best position to negotiate since *she* was the one asking *him* for a favor. She'd do anything to make Grandpapa's last days on earth happy ones...and it wasn't exactly as if it would be a chore. Sebastian was, *ahem*, gorgeous, after all. And why shouldn't she enjoy herself in bed with the rogue for a bit when she was destined to return to her lonely life in the country afterward? Second, it wasn't as if she'd be in any danger of falling back in love with the scoundrel. She'd long ago stopped caring what he was doing, stopped wondering who he was with. She was well and truly over him, and no silly agreement would change that. Third, and most importantly, the moment Sebastian made his request, she'd been overwhelmed by...well, hope was the only word for it. This would be her only chance for a baby. She'd be a fool not to take it. If it gave him what he wanted too, an heir, so be it.

"We should talk," Sebastian's voice nearly startled her.

She lowered her periodical and blinked at him. "Talk? About what?"

He shrugged. "You know? What's been going on in our

lives…in case your grandfather asks a question we cannot answer."

Veronica frowned. "Hmm. You're probably right."

"I'm certain it pained you to admit that," Sebastian replied with a haughty grin.

She rolled her eyes. "Given that I don't care to hear about your conquests with women," she said, trying to keep her lip from curling. "What else have you been up to?"

"Parliament mostly," he replied, obviously ignoring her jab. "And social obligations. Most of them excruciatingly boring. What have you been up to? How are you keeping busy in the country? Done any painting?"

Veronica's chest went tight. Painting? She'd loved to paint when she was a girl. She'd told him that…once, a long time ago. It seemed like a lifetime. She hadn't painted in years, however, and for some reason it made her wistful knowing that he remembered. She'd barely mentioned it. "I don't have any paints," she answered honestly, doing her best to keep all emotion from her voice.

He frowned. "Gardening much?" he asked next, a sly smile on his lips.

She arched a brow at him. She definitely recalled the times she'd told him in no uncertain terms that she didn't understand why anyone would want to root around in the heat and mud all day with bugs crawling about. Jessica adored gardening, but it was not for Veronica and never would be.

"Oh, yes, I spend loads of time gardening," she replied, returning his smile.

"What then? I hope you've found something you enjoy." The sincerity in his voice made her throat go dry.

She nodded hesitantly. "I…I read to the children at the schoolhouse in the village twice a week."

"Read?" He blinked, surprise clearly registered on his face.

"Yes, and two of them, a boy and a girl, are having trouble learning to read. I help them."

"You teach children to read?" He blinked more. His brow was furrowed, as if he didn't understand what she was telling him.

An unexpected smile spread across her face. "You needn't look so shocked. Mr. Trehorn, the schoolmaster, hasn't the time to spend with each one of them individually. So I volunteered. I find I quite enjoy it." She took a breath. "Then, on Wednesdays and Fridays, Mrs. Leggett and I fill baskets with loaves of bread, fruits, and medicines and we take them to the families in the village with sick or ailing members."

"Mrs. Leggett?" Sebastian repeated.

"Yes, the housekeeper at Edgefield Hall. You remember her, don't you?"

"Of course I remember Mrs. Leggett," he replied. "I'm merely trying to picture you and her filling baskets with goods for the villagers."

"Mrs. Leggett is a dear," Veronica said, glancing back down at her periodical. He probably expected Mrs. Leggett to dislike her. But she and the housekeeper had become fast friends. Of course, it had been slightly awkward having to explain why she'd come to Edgefield Hall alone, and even more awkward when the months, then years passed without the arrival of her husband. But Mrs. Leggett made it her practice to be discreet. A quality Veronica cherished in the housekeeper. Veronica was convinced the older woman understood that the subject was a painful one for her. She appreciated the housekeeper's steady presence and unquestioning loyalty.

"What else have you been doing?" Sebastian pressed with genuine interest in his eyes. "I hope you have had no unfortunate encounters with heights."

Veronica snapped up her head. Why did his words make

her heart pound in her chest? Because...he was referring to the night he'd asked her to marry him. They'd been courting for two months. He'd come to Justin's town house in London. Sebastian had tossed pebbles at her second-floor window until she'd opened it. She couldn't help her sigh. She recalled it like yesterday. The fresh June breeze had swept through her window, lifting the wisps of hair at her temples, and ruffling her white, cotton night rail. "What are you doing?" she'd called down to him.

"I need to speak with you," he'd called back. "It's urgent. I'll climb up."

"No!" she'd nearly shrieked, making him freeze.

She quickly shook her head. "I'll come down. I'm terribly afraid of heights, you see. I won't be able to hear a word you say if you're balancing precariously on my window ledge."

She'd hurried downstairs and unlocked the front door as quietly as possible, hoping no servants would awaken to witness her sneak onto the front porch. Thankfully, a large elm tree and a hedgerow covered the space in shadows. No sooner had she made it to the porch than Sebastian had captured her in his arms and pulled her into his embrace for a kiss that left her heady with longing. It wasn't their first kiss, but the one they'd shared that night had been urgent and filled with...tension. Sebastian was nervous, something she'd never felt before from the confident man. She soon learned why.

When the kiss ended, he dropped to one knee, holding her hands in his. "Veronica Marie Kingsley Whitmoreland, will you do me the honor of becoming my wife?"

"Yes!" she nearly shouted before glancing over her shoulder and saying it again in a quieter voice. "Yes, of course I will, Sebastian."

"Thank goodness," he'd breathed. "I have every intention

of asking Justin, of course, to make it official. But I wanted to ask you first…to be certain of your feelings."

The memory made tears fill Veronica's eyes. The look on his face had been so boyish and full of hope. He'd been so caring. So seemingly perfect. Several of her closest friends had already married, and she'd heard the stories of their betrothals over and over. But none of them, not a one, had been asked first by their beau. And certainly not in so romantic a manner. The man had been prepared to climb up to her window, for heaven's sake.

Shaking her head to dispel the unwanted memory, she glanced at him. His gaze captured hers. The periodical slid from her lap. It hit the floor of the coach with a thump and they both leaned over to retrieve it at the same time. His warm hand brushed hers. A spark shot up her arm and a shudder made its way through her body. The lump in her throat grew larger. There had been a time when she had envisioned a full life with this man. When he had made her feel safe, loved. That dream had been dashed, but the memory of it still echoed in her heart. It made her wish for the thing she'd always wanted but knew she couldn't have: the happy marriage her grandparents had been blessed with.

Veronica grabbed the periodical and jolted back upright into a sitting position. She mustn't forget the man was a charmer. The romantic proposal in the moonlight? Dropping to one knee? All the lovely words he'd said… That was Sebastian, wasn't it? He'd convinced not only her but her entire family that he adored her. She'd even believed that he *loved* her. But it had been little more than an act performed to elicit the desired result—her agreement to marry him—before he showed his true colors. He was merely performing his duty…securing a proper wife.

"Do you miss London, Veronica?" His deep voice snapped her from her reverie.

She twisted her head to look out the window. "I miss…" Her voice caught. She stopped and shook her head, willing herself to let go of the daydreams of the past. They weren't real. They never had been. Sebastian wasn't the dream husband she'd thought he was. He was a liar and a cheater. "I quite enjoy my time in the country," she said, her voice flat.

"I see," he replied. She felt his eyes on her, watching her closely. "I enjoy my time in London as well." His voice was equally flat.

Veronica's jaw clenched. She just bet he enjoyed his time in London. Especially the time he spent with his mistress. For all Veronica knew, he had more than one by now. Her nostrils flared, and she returned her attention to the periodical, ripping at the page to turn it. But she wasn't angry at him. She was angry at herself. She'd been momentarily lulled into remembering how he'd courted her. But of course, he'd been on his best, most appealing behavior back then. He'd somehow even managed to keep up the pretense through their honeymoon phase, two entire months. But the fact remained, he'd lied to her. Lied and cheated. Only a fool forgave such things. And she was no fool. That was why she'd insisted there be no kissing. She and Sebastian might be about to spend the next several nights in bed together, but she would *not* fall victim to his considerable charms.

# CHAPTER FIVE

ot an hour later, the coach came to a stop in front of the grand entrance of Whitmore Manor. One of Sebastian's footmen pulled open the door and lowered the steps. Sebastian jumped down first to turn and assist Veronica. As the servants began unloading the trunks from the back of the conveyance, Sebastian braced himself against the icy wind and ushered Veronica to meet her mother, who had materialized at the front door.

Lady Margaret, the Marchioness of Whitmore, was a fine-looking woman; petite with dark hair and eyes, an older version of Veronica. Lady Margaret had always treated Sebastian with respect and kindness, even *after* her daughter had told her the worst about him. Of course, Sebastian didn't know if Justin had attempted to convince his mother that her son-in-law wasn't the scoundrel Veronica believed him to be, not that it was Justin's task to clear Sebastian's name. But if the older woman was angry with Sebastian, she showed no sign of it now. The widow greeted him and smiled warmly. Perhaps she was pretending, too. Perhaps everyone would be pretending this holiday.

After the niceties were exchanged, Sebastian and Veronica were ushered into the house. Inside it smelled like gingerbread, spruce, and burning wood from the many fireplaces, just like Sebastian remembered it. A wave of nostalgia for Christmastides past rolled through him. He'd always had happy times here at Whitmore Manor, much happier than any times he'd had at his own family estate.

Veronica had barely handed her hat, pelisse, and gloves to the butler before she turned to her mother with a worried expression on her face. "How is Grandpapa? May I see him?"

"He's doing well today," Lady Margaret replied.

Veronica visibly exhaled and briefly closed her eyes. "I would like to see him right away."

Lady Margaret nodded. "I'll take you both there now, if you wish," she replied, smiling at Sebastian. "He's been looking forward to seeing you. *Both* of you."

Sebastian narrowed his eyes at Lady Margaret. He had not missed the emphasis she'd placed on the word 'both.' She had to know they were playacting. "Let's go," Sebastian said, managing a smile. "I've missed the old blighter."

Placing his hand on the small of his wife's back, Sebastian ushered her toward the grand staircase. He did not mistake the way Veronica's spine stiffened at his touch, and she did not look at him. Instead, she merely lifted her skirts and followed her mother up the staircase and down the first landing toward the end of the corridor. Sebastian watched her. Her elegant chin arched at an angle but trembling slightly, signifying her apprehension at seeing her grandfather. No doubt she was worried he would be far gone. Sebastian was glad he would be with her when she saw the old duke. She may not relish her husband's company, but she didn't need to be alone at such a time. She loved her grandfather very much.

As they ascended the stairs, Sebastian's mind flashed back

to their conversation in the coach earlier. The image of lovely Veronica reading to a group of school children and teaching two of them to read captured his imagination. She'd wished for four children once upon a time. For the last two years, however, he'd assumed she'd rather go without children than bear *his* children. But now, hearing her talk about the village kids, he wondered…was her desire for children why she'd agreed to his condition so readily?

The idea of Veronica and Mrs. Leggett packing baskets and handing them out in the village was a novel one as well. Mrs. Leggett was a fine judge of character. To hear Veronica tell it, she'd become friendly with the housekeeper. He couldn't quite envision Mrs. Leggett and Veronica together. Was it possible they'd become…friends?

Sebastian's musings were interrupted when their little party arrived at the door to the duke's bedchamber. Lady Margaret knocked once and at a maid's reply, she said, "It's Veronica and Sebastian, Papa. They've come for Christmastide."

"Come in," came the old man's voice.

Lady Margaret pushed open the door and Veronica pulled away from Sebastian's touch to rush directly toward her grandfather's bed. Sebastian followed more slowly, folding his hands behind his back, and strolling toward the enormous bed on the dais, where the old duke lay.

"Grandpapa!" Veronica exclaimed, leaning down to hug the duke the moment she reached him.

"My darling V," the duke said. He wore a burgundy silk dressing gown and sat braced against a veritable mountain of pillows atop the damask bed linens covering the ornate bed.

Sebastian eyed the old man carefully. The Duke of Holden had certainly aged since the last time Sebastian had seen him, but while Sebastian had expected gray skin, protruding bones, and a man who could barely speak, the gentleman before him looked fit with a ruddy, smiling face that was anything but gaunt or pallid.

"Ah, Edgefield," the old duke said, reaching out to shake Sebastian's hand.

Sebastian made his way to Holden's beside and offered his hand. "Your Grace," he said, bowing slightly. "It's been too long."

"Yes, why is that? Why haven't you been coming to our holidays?" Holden asked, his white eyebrows slapped together over his bright blue eyes. "I didn't marry you off to my granddaughter only to see *less* of you, son."

"Oh, Grandpapa, there shall be time to discuss that sort of thing later," Veronica interjected, waving a dismissive hand in the air, though Sebastian noticed she'd gone a shade paler. "Let's just enjoy our time together right now."

"I'm afraid I'm often called to town for Parliamentary purposes, Your Grace," Sebastian lied with a wide smile on his face. "But I'm certainly happy to be here this Christmas-tide with you and Lady Whitmore, and my lovely wife." And with that, he easily pulled Veronica into his arms and gave her a kiss intended to scorch off her boots.

Veronica's entire body quaked. A shudder of pure lust swept through her. She clutched at his sleeves, her head tipping back while Sebastian's tongue mastered her mouth, nearly smoking off her stockings. She clung to him, desperately wanting more, her mind completely blank.

Sebastian deepened the kiss until Veronica was certain she would melt into a puddle on the floor. His bold tongue stroked hers while his hand came up to cup the back of her head and hold her in place. His mouth moved over hers with a skill she had tried to forget, but was remembering now in ways that made heat suffuse her body and settle in the aching spot between her legs.

The sound of Mama clearing her throat made Sebastian

break their contact. He left her standing next to the bed, her lips on fire. She tried to take a step but wobbled, feeling faint. Sebastian's hand moved deftly to steady her elbow. Veronica was limp and speechless. Her breath came in small pants. She quickly glanced at Sebastian and didn't mistake the flare in his eyes as he took a small step back. He was breathless, too. Good. He had been just as affected by their kiss.

She shook her head and reoriented herself to the surrounding scene. She was still standing in Grandpapa's bedchamber and...and... Wait a moment. Sebastian had *promised* not to kiss her. And he'd just broken that promise... in front of her *ailing* grandfather, no less. Why, the man was despicable. That she'd clung to him and enjoyed it had nothing to do with it.

"Well now, young chap," Grandpapa exclaimed with a hearty laugh. "I do hope you'll continue that sort of behavior." He winked at Sebastian. "We need an heir around here in the worst sort of way."

"Grandpapa!" Veronica exclaimed, finding her voice again. She lifted a hand and pressed her finger to her burning lips.

"I quite agree," Sebastian replied to her grandfather, a completely roguish, unrepentant grin on his face. "I shall see to it at my earliest opportunity."

Stifling a gasp, Veronica swiveled sharply on her heel to give Sebastian a warning look outside of her grandfather's sight. Oh, she'd have *plenty* to say to her scoundrel of a husband the moment they were alone together.

Replacing her narrowed-eyed glare for a warm smile, she turned back to her grandfather. "How are you feeling, Grandpapa?" she asked in a desperate bid to change the subject.

"I'm feeling especially fine today," the older man replied, a bright smile on his face. "Now that my V is here, I feel even better." He reached out and patted her hand.

"I'm glad to hear it," Veronica replied, leaning down and pulling the covers over her grandfather's chest. She placed a hand on his leathery cheek. "You're certainly looking fit." She shot a questioning glance at her mother, who merely shrugged.

"He's having a good day. Aren't you, Papa?" Mama interjected.

"Where is Grandmama?" Veronica asked next.

"Her Grace is taking a nap," the maid offered from her spot in the corner where she sat, overlooking Grandpapa's bed.

Veronica nodded. "I look forward to seeing her."

"Speaking of a nap." Grandpapa stretched his arms above his head and let out an exaggerated yawn. "I am feeling tired myself at the moment. I should probably rest before dinner."

"Dinner?" Veronica's brows shot up. She frowned at him. "But, Grandpapa, you cannot possibly mean to come down to dinner."

"I'd like to know why not," Grandpapa replied, his own frowning gaze jumping between Veronica and her mother. "A man's got to eat, doesn't he?"

"Whatever you like, Papa," Mama said, reaching down to pat his hand that rested atop the burgundy coverlet. "We'll leave you to rest now."

Mama quickly ushered Veronica and Sebastian from the room. Veronica didn't speak until they were in the corridor again and many paces away from her grandfather's door. "It can't be good for him to leave bed, can it?"

Mama sighed. "The doctor told us he should be kept comfortable, but allowed to do whatever he seems fit enough to. He's quite excited you're here, darling." She squeezed her daughter's shoulder and gave her an encouraging smile. "I haven't seen him this well in days."

"But he's so ill," Veronica replied, biting her lower lip. "I certainly don't want to be the reason his condition worsens. We should send up a tray." Of course she didn't mention that the more grandfather was around, the more she'd have to pretend to like Sebastian.

Mama chuckled as they began walking back toward the staircase. "I'd like to see you try to keep him away, darling. As you know, he's always been quite stubborn. I'm afraid he's even more so these days."

"I say your grandfather should be allowed to do whatever he likes," Sebastian chimed in as he strolled along beside them.

"I'm not surprised," Veronica replied, giving her husband a tight smile. "You've made it quite clear that you think all men should be able to do whatever they like."

"Ah, ah, ah, my dear," Sebastian replied with a roguish grin on his face, waving one finger back and forth in front of him. "I believe that comment came dangerously close to being rude."

"If you can break the rules, I can too," she shot back with a fake-sweet smile.

Sebastian opened this mouth to retort just as Mama stopped in front of a door to one of the larger guest rooms. "Here we are, dears. I had the maids make up this room for the two of you."

Veronica's head snapped to face her mother. "Perhaps I should stay in my usual room, Mama."

"That wouldn't be proper, would it, dearest?" Sebastian interjected, wrapping an arm around her waist and pulling her against his side in a tight embrace. He batted his eyelashes in an exaggerated manner. "We're married. Of course we'll share a room."

"Sebastian is correct," Mama replied. "You'll stay here. We wouldn't want your grandfather to wonder," she added in a lower tone, a warning expression on her face.

Veronica forced herself to nod, but the moment Sebastian opened the door to the room and splayed his hand wide, allowing her to enter first, the half-hearted smile she'd affected for her mother's sake disappeared.

"Thank you for showing us to our room, my lady," Sebastian said to Mama in his most charming tone, while bowing to her. "We'll see you at dinner."

"Excellent. See you then," Mama replied, trotting off down the hall as if she had no qualms about leaving her daughter in the hands of a cheat and a *double* liar.

The moment the bedchamber door closed behind them Sebastian promptly locked it. Then he leaned back against it, crossed his arms over his chest, and gave her his most roguish grin.

Veronica's breath caught in her throat and a thrill shot through her. *Heaven help me. I'm alone in a bedchamber with a man who could charm the skirts off a saint.*

# CHAPTER SIX

**B**elieving that a good offense would prove to be the best defense, Veronica crossed her arms over her chest and contemplated Sebastian. She couldn't narrow her eyes any farther. It was impossible. "Well?" She tapped a booted foot on the floor.

"Well, what?" he replied, still blinking his dark eyelashes at her as if he were entirely innocent of any misdeeds. He took a seat in a chair near the door and removed his boots.

Her voice was a low growl. "You broke the kissing rule."

"No. I didn't," he announced with a cunning smile. "I never agreed to that rule."

"What?" She resisted the urge to stamp her foot. Though she'd prefer to stamp on *his* foot.

"I agreed to your first rule, but I never agreed to the second," he explained. "I merely replied with my second rule, which you *did* agree to."

Veronica's nostrils flared, and she continued to watch him with a thunderous glare. "You're a villain," she shot out.

"But you already thought that of me," he said, still smiling.

He stood again. "What do I have to lose to sink further in your esteem?"

Veronica cocked her head to the side. "Fine. If you didn't agree to that rule, then I have *two* more rules to make."

Sebastian tipped his head to the side and shrugged. "Seems fair."

"Though why you'd even *want* to kiss me is beyond me." She waved a hand in the air.

She'd said the remark in an offhanded manner, but quickly regretted it when Sebastian stepped forward and leaned down, his mouth hovering near her ear. Gooseflesh popped along her neck, and she tipped her head to the side. His breath was a hot whisper. "It's not possible for me to bed you and *not* kiss you. I simply cannot do it. And if you're honest, you don't want me to."

He pulled her into his arms and pressed his nose along the sensitive skin beneath her ear. The gooseflesh spread all the way down her side, and she shivered.

"I felt you shudder when I kissed you," he continued in the same hot whisper. "I intend to kiss you...*everywhere.*"

Veronica swallowed. Her heart thumped painfully in her chest. She couldn't do this. Not now. Not yet. She quickly pulled out of his arms, rushed to her trunk, opened it, and began pulling out clothing in no particular order. She must unpack. It was time to set the clothes to rights. This was too much. Too much, too fast. They were alone in a bedchamber. She couldn't go to bed with him right now. She needed time to get herself together. Her insides were a mass of nerves. What if it wasn't like it used to be? Or even worse...what if it *was*?

She'd only placed a few items in the wardrobe before she turned to see him silently staring at her, arms crossed over his chest, an amused look on his face.

"Can't Mary see to unpacking your things later?" he

drawled as he removed his coat and tossed it atop a nearby chair. His waistcoat soon followed.

Veronica cleared her throat. Unpacking was giving her something to concentrate on besides remembering the quivers that had invaded her spine when the man had kissed her, something besides the tingle between her legs when he'd glanced his lips along her sensitive neck. Something other than the heat that had suffused her whole body, the shiver that had traced its way along her thighs. His words, his actions, his *undressing*, had completely thrown her off balance. "I'm certain Mary is tired from the long drive," she replied in a far-too-high voice, dedicated to her task...and avoiding him.

"And you're not?" he drawled, pulling off his cravat and tossing it on the chair with his other clothing. Dear God. He was disrobing. *Disrobing*.

"Not partic—" She froze. Drat. She'd walked directly into his trap. She gulped.

"Good. I'm not either. Shall we?" He tipped his head back toward the bed.

Heat spread through her body as if she'd just lowered herself into a steaming bath. Beads of sweat formed between her breasts. She turned away to drop to her knees and rummage through her trunk while she worked to keep her breathing even. "But we just got here. It's the middle of the day." As excuses went, it was particularly lame, but at the moment, it was all she had.

His chuckle followed. He stepped forward, leaned down, and traced a finger along her collarbone. His touch alone made her shiver. He crouched beside her, and his voice was a hot breath in her ear. "I seem to remember on our honeymoon we made love in the middle of the day. Several times."

Veronica froze and briefly closed her eyes. "I know my second rule," she choked out.

"What?" His voice held a note of apprehension.

*"Don't* call it lovemaking," she said through clenched teeth.

He pulled the chemise she was holding from her hands and let it drop back into the trunk. Then he stood and pulled her up with him into his arms. Veronica shuddered again. His mouth dropped to her neck and traced a heated path along the vein that led to her shoulder. Dear God. His tongue lit her up like a line of Christmas candles. When his mouth reached her ear again, he whispered, "I don't care what we call it as long as you come to bed with me. Right. Now."

Trembling with a mixture of trepidation and what she didn't want to admit but knew was desire, Veronica let him lead her to the bed. The large piece of furniture took up the entire center of the room and was covered with a jade-green satin coverlet and stark white sheets.

Sebastian stopped next to the bed and stroked her cheek. "You're beautiful, Veronica."

She sighed and closed her eyes. "And you're handsome. Too bad you're a—"

His mouth swooped down to cover hers, silencing her words. Her head tipped back, and her arms instinctively went around his neck. She anchored herself to him. It felt too good to pull away. And he was right. Damn him. She wanted it. She wanted his kiss. She wanted his touch. It had been too long. She'd been nervous minutes ago, but now all she wanted was to be tangled naked in the bedsheets with him, feeling his muscles ripple beneath her fingertips as he pumped into her.

His mouth moved along her cheek to her ear. He bit the lobe slightly before tracing the tip of his tongue down her neck, across her throat. Then he lowered his head to her *décolletage,* tantalizing her by rubbing the backs of his fingers along her nipples, kissing the exposed tops of her breasts

51

before moving up, sucking at her neck, dipping into the little crevice at her collarbone, lapping at the spot behind her ear that he knew drove her wild. "I can make you burn," he whispered. "I remember how."

"It's been so long," she whispered in a shaky voice just before her gown gave way. She glanced down in surprise. The entire time he'd been touching her, he'd also been unbuttoning the back of her gown. It bunched into a heap around her arms. *Rogues were good for some things*, she thought, just before her knees buckled and he caught her, sweeping her into his arms and laying her atop the mattress. He leaned down, still kissing her, and she wrapped her arms over his broad shoulders and pulled him atop her, desperate to feel his weight. Their kiss turned wild. Her arms linked fiercely around him. She would explode if he didn't enter her at once. He grabbed her shift and pulled it down beneath her breasts, letting his hot mouth suck first one hardened nipple, then the other until she cried out.

Awash in pure desire, Veronica arched her back and slid her fingers through his hair. Her head moved back and forth against the pillow as his tongue on her nipples drove her slowly mad. She shuddered. Her stays were cutting into her ribcage, but she didn't care.

One of his hands moved down to push her shift up her legs and his finger quickly found the spot between her hips where she was desperate for his touch. The moment he touched her, she cried out. She wanted him. So desperately. All of him. Right now.

He shifted his hand between their bodies and unbuttoned his breeches with frantic, unsteady fingers. Freeing himself, he parted her thighs, finding his spot and sliding home deep inside her in one sure, swift thrust. Veronica cried out while a growl was torn from Sebastian's throat as he pumped into her again and again.

SEBASTIAN COULDN'T STOP HIMSELF. He was no longer a man. He'd gone wild, slaking his lust with the woman he'd dreamed about nightly for so long. He was on fire for her, and nothing could stop him. Nothing except a word from her. Only she hadn't stopped him. Instead, her head was thrown back, her eyes were tightly shut, and she was making whimpering noises in the back of her throat that made him want to cum so hard.

But he couldn't. Not yet. They might be pretending this week, but he'd be damned if she pretended in bed. No. Every single one of those little sobs, every clamp of her knees against his hips, every rake of her nails down his back, told him the truth. She wanted this. She wanted him. And she was enjoying it. But he intended to make it even better for her.

Sweat beaded on his brow. "God, I've wanted you…for so. Damn. Long." Each word was punctuated by a long stroke. Every thrust sent a shiver up his spine, one that clutched at his bollocks and made him want to spend himself. But he couldn't. Not yet. Not while she was yet unfulfilled. After all, he wanted her to want more, didn't he? So much more.

VERONICA WAS MINDLESS. She couldn't talk, couldn't think, could only move her hips in time to his thrusts while she struggled for the release she knew he could give her, the release she wanted so badly.

Gasps hitching in her throat, she bit his neck, sucking on the slightly salty skin while his finger moved between them again to rub her in the spot where she wanted it most.

God. What had he just said to her? He'd wanted her for so long? That was hot. She'd be lying to herself if she didn't admit she'd wanted him, too. That she'd laid in bed alone at night at Edgefield Hall, remembering the nights he'd made her body come alive. The way he'd touched her, stroked her, licked her, kissed her until she was a quivering mass of need in his arms and then he'd released her. Let her soar among the clouds, shivers racking her body while he stroked into her and took his own pleasure. She'd missed it. Blast it. She'd missed this. She'd wanted him for so long, too.

"Cum for me, Veronica," he growled in her ear. "Say my name," he demanded.

The pressure built between her legs as he pumped into her and rubbed her until Veronica was a mindless, panting mess. Her thighs quivered, her knees clamped tightly against his hips, and she was making tiny sobs in the back of her throat. "Yes. Yes. Yes," she breathed against his neck over and over before letting her head fall back. And with a keening cry, she called his name while the exquisite feeling overtook her, and her legs trembled before she went limp.

"I'm sorry, love. I can't...stop," he groaned, pumping into her one last time, and growling her name against her rumpled hair before falling to a spent heap atop her.

# CHAPTER SEVEN

Sebastian propped the pillow behind his head and frowned at the far wall of the bedchamber. Immediately after they'd made love, Veronica had called for a bath and disappeared into the next room while the footmen brought up steaming buckets of water. She couldn't even stand to remain in the same room with him while the bath was prepared.

Damn it. He wasn't proud of himself. His performance in bed just now especially. He'd behaved like an untried schoolboy. He hadn't been with a woman—with Veronica—for over two years. And even though he'd told himself repeatedly on the journey here that he would have to think of something else, anything else, in order to control himself, the first time he touched her, the moment his fingers met her soft skin, all of his good intentions flew from his mind. He'd been overcome with lust, completely out of control. It had been far too long.

Veronica had enjoyed herself. He knew that much. She might think the worst of him, but she'd wanted him. She couldn't fake the wetness between her legs or the moans she'd made deep in her throat, and when he'd asked her if she wanted him, he'd seen the truth deep in her dark eyes. And then he'd made her come apart with his finger. He smiled to himself. He'd wanted to do it with his tongue, but there'd be time for that later. Oh, yes. That had been the best part. The way her thighs had quivered. The way her knees had clamped him. The way she'd tossed back her head and raked her fingers through his hair. He could feel the need building inside of her and when she'd found her release, she hadn't been faking that. He could tell she'd found pleasure beneath his touch. They might be estranged, but he wasn't such a scoundrel that he'd forced himself on a woman who didn't truly want him.

He had to wonder, however. Had *she* also been celibate all this time? The way she'd said, "It's been so long," made him wonder. Perhaps she'd meant with *him*, but he hoped she'd meant with *anyone*. He wanted to believe that. Of course, he hadn't ever dared to ask, or to pretend he cared. It was an unspoken rule that she would not produce someone else's bastard and try to pretend as if it was his child, but he hadn't been able to contemplate the idea that she may have been unfaithful. Though she'd been convinced he'd been unfaithful to her, which allowed her an excuse. It was just that...the thought of another man touching Veronica ripped Sebastian apart inside. It made him want to destroy things. He didn't want to contemplate it even now. But something in her demeanor, her words, her uncertainty at first, had told him she'd been untouched all this time. And that thought made him smile, made him breathe a sigh of relief. The woman may not trust him, but God, how he wanted her. Even now. Their lovemaking hadn't slaked his desire. It had only inflamed it. He wanted her again. Already.

A faint noise coming from the bath chamber caught his attention. She was...humming. He grinned, then pushed himself out of the bed, located his breeches, and pulled them on.

Clad only in his breeches, he strolled into the bath chamber, where he stopped near the door and propped his shoulder against the frame, watching her as she soaped a slender arm. "Might it be that our, *ahem*, time in bed this afternoon is the reason for your good mood?"

Her eyes widened, and she dunked beneath the water until the bubbles covered her head. A moment later, she emerged tentatively, ensuring the bubbly water covered her breasts. Such a shame.

"What are you doing in here?" she asked, eyeing him carefully.

He arched a brow. "You object? After what we just did in the bedchamber?"

A shocked smile played across her pink lips, and she splashed water toward him. "This isn't the bedchamber," she answered primly, lifting her nose in the air.

He pushed himself away from the door and stalked toward her, capturing her gaze with his. When he reached the side of the tub, he leaned down and trailed a finger into the steamy water. "Yes, but I also seem to recall a time in Paris when we—"

"Sebastian!" She clutched an arm over her breasts this time.

He chuckled. "Ah, I see you remember it too." He leaned across the tub, bracing a hand on each side and gave her a positively roguish stare. "Baths can be quite amusing with the right partner."

She gave him a condemning glare. "Be that as it may," she said, clearing her throat. "I would like some privacy now, if you don't mind."

"A pity," he said with a sigh before straightening and turning back toward the door. "But I'll go."

Sebastian sauntered back into the bedchamber, retrieved his shirt, and pulled it over his head. Yes, even after their lovemaking—he refused to call it anything else, even if she insisted on it—it was clear his stubborn wife still didn't trust him. He'd told her he hadn't *been* with Melissa, at least not sexually, but Veronica refused to believe it. She had proof of his lie in the form of a note from Melissa. But the fact remained he hadn't touched Melissa since well before his and Veronica's engagement, let alone the wedding. What his stubborn, infuriating wife didn't know was that he actually *had* been madly in love with her. Only he hadn't said it before...before she'd left him. And now he had to live with that regret.

VERONICA WATCHED Sebastian leave the bath chamber and close the door behind him. She couldn't tear her eyes off his enticing backside. The man had been blessed with an unmercifully fit body and this afternoon she'd had the chance to see it once more. See it. Touch it. And *feel* it. A shudder ran down her spine. She hadn't been hallucinating in the bath chamber at his town house the other night. He was godlike and the muscles on his abdomen were even more impressive when she was running her fingers along them.

He was also a master with his fingers and his mouth. That was all there was to it. He'd broken down her defenses and made her feel...everything again in just minutes. But oh, God, the best part. The best part hadn't even been when she'd shattered into a million little pieces against his fingertip...the best part was when he'd pumped into her again and again, sweat beading on his brow, apologizing for his performance because he couldn't control himself. *That* had been the best part, and she'd squeezed him with her inner muscles as tightly as she could while she raked her nails down his strong back because she knew that drove him mad.

It had been...magnificent. Only...she hadn't planned to enjoy herself so much.

Tears sprang to her eyes. But not tears of sadness. Tears of anger. She was angry at herself. It was so good with him. She'd allowed him to break down her defenses so quickly. He'd always been able to do that to her. How? Why? She wanted him with an intensity that frightened her. Again. Already.

Dear God. This was going to be the longest fortnight of her life.

## CHAPTER EIGHT

Over an hour later, Sebastian was finishing his own bath when a knock sounded on the door. His valet entered, bearing a note atop a silver salver.

*I've just arrived. Meet me in the billiards room for a game before dinner.*

The message was unsigned, but Sebastian would know Justin's scrawling handwriting anywhere. Sebastian had seen it often enough during their school days. He hurried through the rest of his dressing. Veronica had already dressed and left. In fact, the moment Sebastian had ordered the tub refilled, she'd made her excuses and fled from the room. No doubt she was downstairs having a pleasant visit with her mother, perhaps her grandmother as well.

By the time Sebastian made it to the billiards' room, dusk had settled over the snowy landscape. The fires had all been stoked, and the icy windowpanes inside the billiards' room reflected the glow.

Sebastian knocked once and at his old friend's reply, he stepped into the room.

"Edgefield," Whitmore called, a bright smile on his face. He was opening an ornate wooden box containing the three ivory billiard balls. "Just in time for me to trounce you before dinner."

"I'm a far better billiards player than you and we both know it," Sebastian shot back with a grin of his own, coming to stand next to his friend and shaking his hand. "Good to see you, Whitmore."

Justin looked too much like his sister. Dark hair, dark eyes, high cheekbones. But Sebastian had known Whitmore since they were children, and while they might look alike, Justin was much less stubborn than his younger sister. He was confident without being arrogant and he was extremely *trusting* of those closest to him...also unlike his sister.

Whitmore requested two glasses of brandy from a footman who stood at the ready while Sebastian strolled up to the billiards table. "Pleasant journey?" he asked, as he picked out his favorite stick from the assortment of finely polished cues and maces that rested against the wall. This wasn't the first game of billiards the two had played in the large room at Whitmore Manor.

"Indeed. I would have asked if you and your fair duchess wanted to share my coach, but I thought perhaps you two might wish to speak...*ahem*...alone."

"Yes, it was probably best we rode separately. You missed hearing your sister take swipes at me the entire journey," he replied, lifting his cue and turning back toward the table.

Whitmore whistled and placed the two white balls and one red one atop the wooden table. "Seriously? She's still angry then. Didn't you explain yourself on the ride here?"

Sebastian groaned and rubbed his free hand through his hair. He and Whitmore had had this conversation many times in the last two years…though usually when they were in their cups. "I did *not* explain myself and I have no intention of doing so. I told your sister what happened that night and she chose not to believe me. There's nothing left to say."

Whitmore sighed, inspecting the leather tip on the end of his cue. "I cannot believe I'm about to say this," he began with a wince, "but tell me again *precisely* what happened."

Sebastian rolled his eyes and placed a fist on his hip. "You've heard it all before."

"I know, but it's been a while. I may have forgotten a significant point that my dear sister ought to be reminded of." He straightened again and gestured to Sebastian to begin the play. "Dukes first," he said with a grin.

"Same rules as usual?" Sebastian asked before leaning down to steady his cue to take the first shot at sinking both Whitmore's white cue ball and the red object ball.

"Same," Whitmore replied with a nod.

Sebastian took the shot and easily sank both balls into the far pocket.

Whitmore stepped over to the pocket to retrieve the balls.

"You might as well save your breath," Sebastian continued. "I doubt she'd listen to you any more than she'll listen to me."

"I am *persona non grata* where my sister is concerned," Whitmore agreed. "But humor me."

Sebastian sighed and took a sip from the brandy glass the footman had just delivered. "Very well. Not two months after Veronica and I married, Melissa—"

"Your mistress," Whitmore pointed out, arching a brow at his friend.

"My *former* mistress sent me a note implying she was with child."

"And you didn't believe her?" Whitmore asked, leaning over the table to take his first shot.

"I was highly skeptical since I hadn't been with her for months...since I began courting your sister, *and* because Melissa hadn't accepted my decision to dispense with our arrangement with grace."

"She was peeved," Whitmore interpreted as he shot the red object ball into the nearest pocket.

Winning, Sebastian smiled and shook his head. "More like enraged. She'd been sending me angry letters all summer. After the first few, I stopped reading them. Threw them directly in the fireplace."

Whitmore narrowed his eyes at Sebastian, who'd retrieved the object ball and had bent to take his second shot. "What made you read the one she sent two months after the wedding, then?"

"That's just it," Sebastian replied, sending his cue ball cracking against the object ball, which dutifully dropped into the pocket. "The letters had stopped before the wedding. It had been weeks since I'd received one. I thought perhaps she'd come around to see reason. Instead, I was disconcerted to read that she was claiming to be with child and that the babe was undoubtedly mine."

"You had no choice but to go see for yourself," Whitmore offered.

Sebastian sighed and stood up straight again. "Yes. Damn my morals to hell. If on the slight chance she *was* with child, *my* child, I, of course, would do the right thing by her and provide for her and babe. Only I had no intention of doing so without seeing for *myself* that she was, indeed, with child. She'd lied to me before and was prone to dramatics. I didn't put it past her to dissemble to attract my attention, either. I had been ignoring her after all."

"So, you went to her town house," Whitmore continued.

Sebastian took another sip of brandy and shook his head, staring unseeing out the darkened windows into the snowy night. "Worst mistake I've made, and that includes the time you and I thought it would be a lark to fill Chancellor Hawkings' bedchamber with honey and let bees loose inside."

"Nearly got expelled from Eton," Whitmore replied with a laugh and a wince.

"Nearly got beaten to death by my father," Sebastian replied grimly, taking another sip.

"The moment you saw Melissa, you knew she'd been lying?" Whitmore probed, taking the next shot, which merely sent both Sebastian's cue ball and the object ball flying.

"Oh, she tried hard enough," Sebastian replied. "She'd tucked sheets under her skirts and pretended she had to remain abed because of the doctor's instructions. But I quickly exposed her scheme by asking her some pointed questions about how far along she was and doing the maths in my head. She was flustered, and I pulled the sheets out from under the bedclothes. She admitted she'd invented the entire tale."

Whitmore clucked his tongue and shook his head, taking a sip from his brandy glass. "One wonders what was going through her mind. Did she think you'd never realize she'd lied?"

"God knows," Sebastian replied. "I'd like to think she would have staged some sort of accident that would account for her plausibly losing the babe, but I can't say I've never wondered if she would have tried to procure an actual child somehow. Makes me shudder to think of it. At any rate, you can see why I didn't tell my *wife* that I had a plan to visit my former mistress to determine if she was lying about being pregnant with *my* child."

Whitmore winced again and sucked in his breath. "Yes, I can't imagine that would have gone over well in your household."

Sebastian shook his head. "Of course, I had no intention

of mentioning it to Veronica if it turned out to be nothing. Only when I returned home and she asked me where I had been, I replied that I'd been at the club. Which was true because I had met you there later."

"But...?" Whitmore prodded, lifting both brows.

Sebastian expelled his breath. "But I didn't know Melissa had a note delivered to Veronica the moment I'd left home, informing Veronica that I could be found in Melissa's bedchamber that evening."

Whitmore's face crumpled into a deep frown. He shook his head. "Melissa is bold. I'll give her that."

"I had a much worse word for her in mind when I found out," Sebastian said with a tight smile. "At any rate, I stepped directly into the trap Melissa had set. Veronica showed me the note and asked me to deny that I'd been at Melissa's house. I could not. I tried to tell her that nothing had happened, but it was too late. I'd been caught in a lie and—"

"And my sister still hasn't forgiven you," Whitmore finished.

"Precisely," Sebastian said. "Unfortunately," he added with a grumble, "she's refused to believe me all this time. She's made her choice."

"She never even listened to your explanation?" Whitmore asked.

"Oh, she listened all right. She listened and then promptly told me she didn't believe me. That's when I stopped trying to explain myself."

"And that's why you didn't try to stop her when she left you?"

A thunderous look covered Sebastian's face. "I wasn't about to have a sham of a marriage with a woman who refused to trust me."

"But you *had* lied to her?" Whitmore clarified. "And been caught in the lie?"

Sebastian's nostrils flared, and he stamped his cue against the floor. "Yes, but—"

"No. No. Simply clarifying," Whitmore replied, bending to take his next shot.

"She refused to give me the benefit of the doubt," Sebastian said, wanting to grind his cue directly into the earth.

Whitmore scratched the back of his neck. "You must admit, the doubt looked extremely doubtful. What *was* she to think?"

Sebastian narrowed his eyes. "Whose side are you on, Whitmore?"

"That's just it," Whitmore replied with a long sigh. "I'm on no one's side. Or both sides, if you prefer."

"That's utterly useless of you," Sebastian declared with a reluctant grin.

"I haven't changed my stance on this in the past two years, Edgefield. Despite the fact that my own sister has nearly disowned me for not taking *her* side."

Sebastian shrugged. "Yes, well, she's unreasonable. That's hardly your fault."

Whitmore braced a hip against the table. "Perhaps. But you must recall my first inkling of your little drama was when Veronica came to visit me the next morning—woke me up from a sound slumber, I might add—to ask me if I had, in fact, been at the club with you the night before."

Sebastian rubbed the back of his neck. "Yes, and you said you were."

"Yes, but then she asked if I knew whether you'd gone elsewhere before the club."

"She had no right to ask you that," Sebastian insisted.

"Regardless, I said I was not at liberty to share my closest friend's secrets with anyone, even my sister."

"And she's been angry with you ever since," Sebastian replied, bending to take his next shot. "See? Unreasonable."

"Perhaps." Whitmore shrugged.

"And now we're here—she and I—pretending we can stand the sight of each other, for your grandfather's sake," Sebastian added.

Whitmore chuckled. "Yes, well. Unfortunately, my sister inherited our grandfather's stubbornness. It won't be easy to convince her to see reason."

"Precisely why I've stopped trying," Sebastian replied before pulling out his timepiece and consulting it. "I suppose we should go to dinner. We can finish this game later. I believe we are tied."

"Yes, to both," Whitmore replied, setting his cue against the wall. "Let's go. I cannot wait to watch Veronica *pretend* to be nice to you."

## CHAPTER NINE

Veronica was seated between Sebastian and her brother at the dinner table. Mama was at the end of the long expanse, while Grandmama sat on her right and Grandpapa on the left. Elizabeth and Jessica sat next to Grandpapa, while Veronica and the two men sat next to Grandmama. Veronica and her brother had exchanged a strained greeting and Jessica had been chattering nonstop since they'd all taken their seats.

"Tell me again what it's like at the queen's court for the debut ceremony," Jessica insisted, her eyes fixed on Veronica.

"I've told you a dozen times," Veronica said with a laugh. "It's all quite formal and nerve-inducing, but thankfully, it's over rather quickly."

"I've been practicing all my dances," Jessica replied, a dreamy look in her dark eyes. "The waltz is my favorite. Isn't it, Grandpapa?" she asked, turning to him.

"Yes, darling, and your waltz is lovely," Grandpapa said, raising his glass in a silent toast to his granddaughter.

Veronica shot a worried glance at her mother. Surely, Grandpapa shouldn't be dancing with Jessica in his condition. But knowing her grandfather, he'd no doubt insisted. The old man was stubborn to a fault. Mama's answer was merely a shrug.

"What about you, Elizabeth?" Veronica asked next, turning toward her second sister. "What is your favorite dance?" She was quite enjoying talking to her younger sisters, partly because she hadn't seen them in several months and she missed them, and partly because Jessica's chatter was keeping her from having to exchange any awkward conversation with Sebastian for Grandpapa's sake.

"None of them," Elizabeth replied in her characteristic monotone. Poor Elizabeth. She'd rather be reading in the library than dancing, and they all knew it.

"How can you say that?" Jessica said to her twin with a sorrowful look on her face. "Dancing is one of the most amusing things we've learned so far. And we'll get to do so with handsome gentlemen next spring. I cannot wait." She pressed her hands together near her cheek. "Though we can only hope there is a gentleman for each of us as eligible and handsome as our dear Sebastian," she added with a laugh.

Sebastian's brows rose, and he inclined his head in a gracious nod before lifting his glass toward Jessica. "A most exquisite compliment, Lady Jessica," he replied. "If only your sister thought as much of me," he added under his breath, but Veronica did not miss it.

"What was that?" she shot at him, watching him from the corners of her eyes.

"Nothing, dearest," he replied with a wide smile, taking a sip from his wine glass.

"Yes, well, I, for one, would like to hear from the newly-weds," Justin interjected, just as the first course of turtle soup was being served.

Danger bells sounded in Veronica's head. Justin was up to

something. She could feel it. He liked nothing better than to rile her.

"You are still considered newlyweds, are you not?" Justin continued, turning first to Veronica, then to Sebastian, and blinking innocently at them.

"No, not at all," Veronica replied, doing her best to keep a false smile pinned to her lips for Grandpapa's sake. "We've been married for over two years. I'm certain there's nothing interesting we can tell you. Our lives are quite dull. Aren't they, Sebastian?" She finished with an edge to her voice, warning her husband to answer in the affirmative before she took a sip of wine.

"Oh, I don't know," Sebastian replied, settling back into his chair as if he relished the conversation. "I'd say our married life of late has been more interesting."

Veronica choked on her wine. A coughing fit ensued that forced Sebastian to slap her on the back. The moment she'd regained her composure, she swiftly kicked his leg under the table.

"Ouch." Sebastian leaned down to rub his leg, wincing.

Meanwhile, Veronica gave her brother a look intended to indicate he'd be kicked next if he didn't quickly change the subject.

"If you've nothing to report," Justin replied with an innocent smile, "then perhaps Grandpapa and Grandmama may answer my questions."

"What would you like to know, dear?" Grandmama asked in her sweet, cheerful voice, her dark eyes sparkling.

"I'm curious," Justin replied. "What do you find to be the secret to such a long and clearly happy marriage?"

Grandmama smiled and laughed. "Oh, well, first, it hasn't been happy *every* day. That I can assure you. But most days we're quite content, wouldn't you say, Arthur?"

"Best decision I ever made, asking your grandmother to

marry me," Grandpapa replied, lifting his glass in a salute to his wife.

A lump formed in Veronica's throat and a smile touched her lips. Her grandparents were lovely. They deserved their happiness. Too bad it was too late for her and Sebastian.

"Yes, but what's the *secret?*" Justin prodded. "What advice can you offer those of us who've yet to reach such a milestone?"

Grandmama's brow creased as she appeared to contemplate the question for a moment. "I suppose listening to one another and admitting when we are each wrong have been instrumental in our happiness. It doesn't hurt that I still find your grandfather as handsome as the day I met him." She glanced over at her husband with a decided twinkle in her eye.

"I feel the same," Grandpapa replied, winking at his wife. "I would also add that keeping a sense of humor helps quite a bit."

"Ah, so listening to each other and keeping your humor," Justin replied, lifting a spoonful of soup to his lips. Once he'd swallowed, he continued, "Would you also say *trust* was important?"

Veronica clenched her jaw. She turned to give Justin another tight smile. He wasn't fooling her. She knew precisely what he was doing.

"Oh, yes," Grandmama replied. "Trust is of the *utmost* importance."

"Trust, even when things look bad?" Justin prodded, blinking innocently.

"Especially then," Grandpapa added.

Sebastian cleared his throat. "You should tell your granddaughter. I've found she is *quite* mistrustful."

Veronica swung her leg to deliver another swift kick to

Sebastian's, but found that he'd already moved it. He grinned at her in triumph.

She cleared her throat and lifted her chin. "I believe *fidelity* is important as well. Would you not say, Grandmama?"

Grandmama began nodding. "Yes, dear, *ever* so important. I know many ladies of the *ton* aren't concerned with such things, but I could not have endured infidelity."

"What's infidelity?" Jessica piped up.

"Never you mind, dear," Mama replied to the girl, while Veronica and her mother exchanged a look.

"Surely, fidelity goes hand-in-hand with trust, though, doesn't it?" Justin asked Grandmama.

That was it. Veronica had had enough of her brother's needling. Before Grandmama had a chance to reply, Veronica turned to her brother and said, "I'm pleased to see you taking such an interest in marriage, Justin. I daresay you should think about your *own* marital prospects. You *are* the Whitmore heir, after all." Veronica finished with an extremely smug smile on her face, directed squarely at her brother.

"Yes," Mama interjected with a firm nod. "Your sister makes an excellent point."

"Indeed, she does," Grandpapa added. "Why haven't you taken a wife yet, Justin? It's high time, my boy."

Behind her wine glass, Veronica smiled widely at Justin, who returned her look with a narrowed-eyed glare of his own. They both knew there was nothing Mama and Grandpapa liked to discuss more than Justin's intentions of finding a bride.

"Indeed," Justin replied, clearing his throat and squaring his shoulders. "How do you all know I don't intend to find a bride next Season?"

"Do you?" Mama's brows shot up. A look of hope enveloped her face.

"Do you?" Grandpapa's voice was equally hopeful.

"Do you?" Veronica and Sebastian chimed together, their voices dripping with skepticism.

"Do you?" Jessica echoed, eagerly.

"Do you?" Elizabeth scrunched up her nose and frowned.

"Don't look so surprised, everyone," Justin replied with a laugh. "Perhaps that's why I'm *asking* these questions. To prepare myself."

"Oh, I'm so pleased to hear that," Mama replied, a radiant smile on her face.

Veronica narrowed her eyes at her brother. He'd won this round. Justin was the consummate bachelor. He had absolutely no intention of taking a wife anytime soon, and they both knew it. He was giving Mama and Grandpapa false hope only to rile her, the rogue.

"Yes, now I have several more questions about what makes a happy marriage," Justin replied, smirking at Veronica. "Shall I continue?"

## CHAPTER TEN

Later that night, after the twins and Grandmama had taken their leave from the drawing room where the ladies had retired after dinner, Veronica sat alone in the silence sipping tea with her mother.

"Grandpapa looks well," she remarked.

"He does, doesn't he?" Mama replied. She was sitting across from Veronica by the crackling fire, a fur covering her lap.

Veronica sat in silence for a few more moments before summoning the nerve to ask her mother a question she'd wanted to ask her for an age. "Why did you do it, Mama? Why did you tolerate Father's cheating?"

Mama's eyes flared before they settled back down and took on a resigned look. "I didn't know you knew about that, Veronica," she breathed.

Veronica pushed herself to the edge of her seat. "Of course I knew. We all did. At least Justin and I did. We heard the fights."

Mama's gaze met Veronica's and pain was clearly etched

deeply in her countenance when she replied. "I'm sorry you heard that."

"I know he hurt you, Mama. Why didn't you send him away? Why did you keep welcoming him back into your home, into your be—?" She stopped herself. She was crossing a line. Letting her anger control her.

"It's not that simple, darling," Mama replied quietly. "I loved him."

"Exactly, which is why—" Veronica stopped herself again. She'd been about to say, "which is why I never let myself love Sebastian." Tears filled her eyes. She could still hear her father's raised voice. "*I promise you, Margaret, it won't happen again. You have my word.*"

The first time she'd heard him say those words, Veronica had been filled with relief. Mama had stopped crying, and they'd enjoyed themselves for the rest of the time Father was at the manor. But it soon became apparent that her father had no intention of keeping his word. He left his family in the country to see to business in London, and every time he returned, the fights would happen again. Veronica had listened with rage in her childish heart, wanting nothing more than to rush to her Mama's side and demand that her father relinquish his mistress. The woman he and Mama had so many rows over.

"You promised, Alistair," Mama always said, her sobs making Veronica's heart ache.

Justin had listened, too. But he'd had more of a resigned, stoic demeanor. He didn't get angry the way Veronica had. They'd both been forced to listen to their parents' raised voices until their governess had stood and closed the door to the nursery.

Nothing ever changed. Father made a lot of promises and went back to London, leaving Mama with a broken heart. Then he'd return, and another fight would ensue. And every time they raised their voices, Veronica promised herself that she'd never allow a man to treat her that way. She'd never welcome a man who'd betrayed her into her bed. She'd never understood how Mama could bear it, especially when Mama had been raised by Grandpapa and Grandmama, who were clearly a lifelong love match.

Veronica closed her eyes. The memory of the night of her first ball after her debut drifted through her mind. Grandpapa had been there, dressed in his best evening clothes. Looking as dapper and handsome as any of the young bucks. He'd proudly escorted his eldest granddaughter into the Cranberrys' ballroom. "Remember," he said with such earnestness in his eyes, "when evaluating a young man, you must ensure he is solid. The type of man who won't let his family down. The type of man who is faithful and cherishes his wife the way I cherish your grandmother."

"A man unlike Father," Veronica had whispered.

Regret had filled her grandfather's eyes. "I begged Margaret not to marry him," he breathed.

Tears had filled Veronica's eyes that night as well. She'd patted her grandfather's hand. "Don't worry, Grandpapa. If I can find a man even half as good as you, I shall count myself fortunate indeed."

"Only the best will do for you, my darling V," Grandpapa had said before the Cranberrys' butler had announced them and he'd escorted her into the dazzling ballroom.

Fear had taken hold of Veronica that night and it had remained her constant companion for the next four Seasons. She danced with a thousand young gentlemen. She'd taken their calls. Accepted their flowers. She'd gone riding in the park with them. She'd allowed them to escort her to Gunter's for a sweet. She'd tried and tried to find the perfect man, one she could love and trust. But her fear of making the wrong choice, of choosing a man like her father, had left her paralyzed with doubt.

That, and the fact that her heart had been captured long ago...by Sebastian Sinclair.

Sebastian had been busy taking over the responsibilities of the dukedom after his father's untimely death. For years, Sebastian hadn't been to any of the balls and soirees and picnics and other parties the rest of the *ton* enjoyed during the Season. It wasn't until Veronica's fifth Season when she was quickly approaching 'on the shelf' by anyone's standards, that Sebastian had returned to Society. And the moment he asked her to dance at the Dunwoodys' ball...her heart was lost.

Of course, Grandfather had given his blessing. He'd been taken in by Sebastian's charm. And it wasn't until it was too late that Veronica had learned the truth.

"You were going to say something else?" Mama gently prodded from her chair across from Veronica.

Veronica opened her eyes again and nodded. "It's just that...I cannot abide cheating," she finally replied, a fierce note in her voice.

"I don't blame you, darling," Mama said, nodding. "It broke my heart."

"But you had a choice, you could have—" Veronica swallowed. There was no use blaming and judging her mother. The woman had been through enough and her husband was dead. It didn't matter that Mama hadn't sent Father away, hadn't forced him to stay in London far away from their family. Veronica had separated herself from her husband, but Mama was different. Veronica would do well to remember that.

"I'm sorry, Mama." Veronica stood and walked to her mother. She leaned down and kissed her mama's forehead. "I only want this holiday to be happy for Grandpapa. I'm going to bed." She turned and made her way toward the door.

"Veronica." Her mother's voice stopped her.

"Yes?" she replied, turning halfway.

"Thank you for bringing Sebastian. I hope you'll find it in your heart to give him a second chance."

Veronica swallowed the lump in her throat. Her poor sweet mother didn't understand. Perhaps she never would. Mama had given Father what felt like a hundred chances. He'd never changed. "Sebastian had his chance, Mama," Veronica replied softly, before striding from the room.

# CHAPTER ELEVEN

After leaving the drawing room, Veronica's pace slowed. She nearly dragged her feet along the runner that led down the corridor toward the grand staircase. But no amount of dawdling could keep her from the bedchamber she shared with Sebastian all night.

Sebastian had already gone up. She knew as much when she walked past the dining room where the men had been left to their port. The room was empty and dark. Of course, it was possible that Sebastian had returned to the billiards' room with Justin, but somehow, she doubted it. She wouldn't be that fortunate.

Reluctantly, Veronica made her way up the staircase. When she finally entered the bedchamber, Sebastian was nowhere to be found, but Mary was waiting for her in the connected dressing room. Veronica entered the dressing room and removed her clothing as slowly as possible. But again, it was no use. Eventually, wearing her dressing gown, she was forced to return to the bedchamber, where her husband had materialized. He was propped up in bed, pillows behind his head, shirt off, and God-knew-what-else off beneath the covers. In addition to the fire in the fireplace, a pair of candles burned on the mantel across the room, casting the room in a shadowy glow. It was *almost* romantic.

As Mary took her leave, Veronica dragged her bare feet along the rug, making snail-like progress toward the bed. She averted her gaze, trying to ignore the tantalizing sight of Sebastian's bare, muscled chest. She climbed atop the mattress and pulled the covers to her neck, then turned to face the wall.

"Good night," she chimed in as pleasant a voice as she could muster, scrunching her eyes closed.

"Good night?" Sebastian echoed, his voice filled with surprise. "Is the evening over, then?"

"I'm quite tired," she insisted, faking a yawn. "It's been a long day."

He rolled toward her and leaned over her, his breath a fiery brand on her neck. "So, you don't want me to do this?" He kissed her neck.

She kept her eyes closed, desire already streaking through her. She loved it when he kissed her neck.

"Or this?" He nipped her earlobe. She loved it when he nipped her earlobe.

She rolled onto her back, already wanting him, her breath coming in hot pants. He moved atop her, his arms braced on either side of her body. "Or this?" he said before leaning down and kissing her deeply.

Veronica was lost. She couldn't resist him and didn't want to. She wrapped her arms over his broad shoulders, reveling in the feel of the sinewy muscle beneath her fingertips. His skin was smooth and firm and hot. His mouth shaped hers, stoking desire throughout her body that pooled in the intimate spot between her legs.

Sebastian pulled his mouth away and moved down. Pushing the covers aside, he slid her night rail up her thighs.

"Or this," he breathed as the fabric slowly ascended to her hips.

Veronica's breath caught. Oh, God. He was going to— And she wanted him to...desperately. But she *shouldn't* want him to...should she?

"I just thought of my third rule," she managed, trying to control the panic rising in her throat.

"Too late," he breathed hotly against her inner thigh before bending to his task.

"What? Why?" But her hands were already fisting the sheets and she didn't give a toss about the third rule.

Sebastian lifted his dark head. "*My* third rule is that you cannot make *your* third rule while we're in the middle of, *ahem*, this."

Veronica's head fell back onto the pillow. His breath was at the juncture between her hips. His arms wrapped around her thighs, and he pulled her legs apart, opening her for him. Then his hot tongue lavished her. She whimpered in the back of her throat, unable to stop herself from making the noise. This, *this* had been something she'd tried to forget, tried and failed. The man could do things with his tongue that made her positively wild with wanting. There was a part of her that realized she hadn't used one of her rules to stop this before because she'd known deep down how much she wanted it, how much she'd missed it.

The third rule should be that he could never stop.

He licked her in long, commanding strokes, all the while holding her thighs apart so she couldn't close herself to him. Not that she wanted to. On the contrary, she wanted exactly what he was giving her, building her toward a climax unlike one she'd had in...far too long.

He sucked her, drawing the small nub into his scorching mouth, and licking it again and again, rolling his tongue over it until her back arched off the bed and her hands clawed at his shoulders, demanding her release.

It came with a force she wasn't prepared for, ripping a keening cry from her throat as her hips fell back to the mattress.

A few moments later, in a delicious fog, she looked down to see Sebastian staring up at her with a smug smile on his lips. He moved back up her body, taking her shift with him. He pulled it over her head and tossed it on the floor. He paused, letting his eyes skim over her naked form. Then he pushed her legs apart with a strong knee and entered her in one swift thrust that made Veronica cry out again in pleasure.

"Tell me you want me," he demanded in her ear as he slowly pulled out and thrust in again.

"I want you," she admitted, already feeling the pressure build again as he slowly maneuvered his hips against hers.

"I want you, too. So much," he groaned as he increased the tempo.

She wrapped her arms around his neck and her hips met his, thrust for thrust, until she was wild again. His hand moved swiftly between their bodies to find that sweet spot once more. He rubbed her, sending her over the edge for the second time before he took his pleasure, thrusting into her one last time before shuddering inside of her, her name a growl in his throat.

Sebastian rolled away from her, but he grabbed her hand, holding it and bringing it to his lips to kiss in a sweet gesture that made unexpected tears spring to her eyes. How was he able to break through her defenses so easily? So quickly? So completely?

"You're holding my hand?" she finally ventured once their breathing had returned to rights.

"Yes, do you object?" came his reply in the candlelight.

"No," she said simply, not entirely certain how she felt about it...or how she should feel.

"I've missed you, Veronica."

Her breath caught. What was he doing? The sex had been intimate enough. But this...*this*. Why was he doing this?

"I want you by my side," he continued.

The lump that had formed in her throat was so large she couldn't swallow. She lay there, staring unseeing at the shadowy ceiling, thinking of the lovely dream that had shattered so many months ago. She closed her eyes, the pain nearly palpable. *He missed her? He wanted her by his side?* His words made her wish for things, wish it could be as simple and lovely as the picture he painted with those two short sentences. As if they could just pretend none of it had happened and they were still the couple they had briefly been once. But his words were too similar to the ones she'd heard Father say to Mama a hundred times. They couldn't just pretend none of it had happened...could they? She closed her eyes and just for a moment, a second or two, she let herself pretend she was already with child from their lovemaking. What if they truly had the family and the life she'd thought they would have when they first married? What if they weren't pretending? How wonderful would that be?

"It's difficult to navigate social obligations without my duchess." His voice came out of the shadows, dragging her back to reality.

Anger slowly seeped through Veronica's body, quickly replacing all the delicious pings from moments before. Social obligations? Ah, yes. How could she forget? That's what he cared about? Not her. Just 'his duchess.' The woman he'd installed in that role just happened to be her. Veronica pushed herself up against the pillows, pulling the covers over her body. "How unfortunate that it's difficult for you to live with the consequences of your actions," she said, pressing her lips together tightly.

"*The consequences of my actions?*" Frowning, he pulled himself up to sit against the pillows on his side of the bed. "Damn it, Veronica, I told you I did not bed Melissa that night. I—"

"You've never understood." Veronica's voice shook with anger. Her dark hair fell over her shoulders. "Even if I believed you, which I *don't*. You *lied* to me. You broke your word. Trust is important in a relationship. You heard my grandparents say so tonight. How could I ever trust you again?"

Sebastian cursed under his breath. His gaze caught hers and held for a few silent moments. Finally, he tossed back the covers, stood, and grabbed his sapphire robe from the back of a nearby chair. Pulling on the garment and belting it, he stalked from the room.

Veronica sat in silence, staring at the door that had just closed behind him. Why was everything between them so complicated? Why couldn't he understand that trust was the foundation of a good marriage and he'd broken that foundation...taken an ax to it? The worst part was, she should have known better. She'd been told plainly enough. She had only herself to blame for not listening.

She closed her eyes and leaned back against the headboard. The memory of the morning after her wedding overtook her. She'd been filled with joy that morning. She'd climbed out of bed, where she and Sebastian had made love all night, and hurried downstairs to see the sunrise over the gardens at Whitmore Manor.

It was her favorite spot and her favorite time of day. Only that morning...she hadn't been alone. Her mother-in-law, the dowager Duchess of Edgefield, had materialized beside her in the early morning light.

She'd only met the woman the night before and had spent little time with her. Veronica got the impression from Sebastian that he didn't particularly want her to spend much time with his mother. Anything he said about the woman was short and emotionless. In all the years she'd known him, Sebastian had never said much about either of his parents, actually. And he changed the subject whenever she'd asked about either of them. She'd got the impression from Justin that Sebastian's father had been a harsh, exacting man. But she heard practically nothing about his mother. She'd told herself if there was something important to know, Sebastian would have told her. But it hadn't stopped Veronica from being exceedingly curious about his mother. Which is why Veronica had been filled with nerves that morning, wanting so badly to make a good impression on Sebastian's only remaining family member.

The dowager was beautiful, with dark black hair and sparkling emerald eyes. Her age hadn't diminished her beauty one whit.

"Good morning, Your Grace," the lady had said as she came to stand next to Veronica. Delight had shot through Veronica. She'd already forgotten that she was a duchess and would be referred to as 'Your Grace' by most everyone.

"I love the sunrise," Veronica had said, a huge smile on her face.

"How charming," the dowager had drawled. "Young people are so full of optimism."

Veronica had frowned, not exactly certain how to reply to that. She'd hoped Sebastian's mother would be content with quietly watching the sunrise since that was what she preferred, but the dowager hadn't remained silent for an entire minute before she said, "I want you to know something, my dear." A serious look had fallen over the woman's face and a knot formed in Veronica's middle.

"My husband, the late duke, wasn't faithful to me a day of our marriage."

Veronica had been forced to stifle a gasp. Why was the duchess sharing such intimate information with her?

"I see," was all Veronica had managed to croak, but a thousand thoughts were already racing through her head. Awful memories of her parents' fights, her mother's sobs.

"It was quite painful," the dowager continued. "He had a mistress. One he never relinquished."

Veronica had wanted the ground to open and swallow her. All she could do was nod. Was it possible the dowager knew about her own father's infidelity? Or was it merely that most men cheated? Most men except Grandpapa...and Sebastian, of course.

"You should know..." the duchess had continued, a pinched, angry look on her face. "Sebastian has a mistress."

In that moment, time stopped. The breath was stolen from her lungs and Veronica began shaking so violently she had to move over a few steps to place a trembling hand on the stone wall that surrounded the garden. She turned to stare at the duchess, unblinking. She wanted to say something, anything, but it felt as if she'd been punched directly in the gut and words had failed her.

"Her name is Melissa," the duchess offered next.

It felt as if Veronica's stays were slowly pressing the life from her body. Was Sebastian's mother truly informing her that her son would not be faithful? Had Veronica just made a terrible mistake marrying him? "No. No. Not Sebastian," she'd finally said. But she wasn't entirely certain if she was defending him or trying to convince herself.

"Don't believe me? Ask him. And if I were you," the duchess continued, "I would secure Sebastian's promise...*immediately*...to rid himself of her. Put your foot down now or you'll end up like I did. Heartbroken. And alone."

Thankfully, a pair of wedding guests had entered the garden just then and the four of them were forced to exchange greetings. Veronica had used the interruption to make her excuses and flee back into the house, but she'd spent the rest of the day mortified, barely able to speak more than a word or two as she and Sebastian spent the day saying good-bye to their many guests.

Veronica had spent hours dwelling on it, wondering if it could be true and what she should do about it. She'd never *asked* Sebastian if he would be faithful. She'd just...assumed it. They'd been so happy together. So...seemingly...in love. And Grandpapa had approved of him. She'd even asked her grandfather the night Sebastian had proposed. "Am I making the right choice, Grandpapa? I'm frightened."

The old man had nodded and hugged her. "You're making an excellent choice, V. You couldn't pick a finer man. I've known Sebastian since he was a boy." They'd all known him since he was a boy. He was Justin's closest friend. He wasn't an adulterer, was he? Until this moment, she hadn't known he'd been a man with a mistress, either. What else didn't she know about him?

Finally, that night after their wedding, after Veronica and Sebastian had ushered the last guests to their coach, Veronica had decided she would simply speak to her husband directly. She would ask him if what his mother had said was true and inform him she would not countenance a mistress.

Veronica waited until they were alone in their bedchamber that evening. He'd pulled her into his arms, but before he could begin kissing her neck, which she'd already learned drove her immediately wild, she stopped him.

"Who is Melissa?" she'd asked pointedly, looking him directly in the eye, watching him closely for his reaction.

The color immediately drained from Sebastian's face, and he stepped back. Nausea had seeped into Veronica's belly. Was this why Sebastian hadn't wanted Veronica to meet his mother before the wedding? And why the devil hadn't *Justin* told her?

"Where did you hear that name?" Sebastian asked, a thunderous look on his face.

Veronica had swallowed hard but held her ground. She was determined to be clear about her conditions. "That hardly matters. Is it true? *Is* she your mistress?"

"She *was* my mistress," Sebastian replied curtly.

Veronica had nearly doubled over. Sebastian had a mistress? Her Sebastian? The man she'd loved since she was a girl? The man she'd just taken vows with the day before? "I demand you get rid of her," Veronica replied next, shaking with nerves. She hadn't intended to sound so imperial, but she was shaking with fear. If he said no...if he refused...she would be forced to...to what? They were already married. She would just have to separate herself from him, exactly the way she'd always wanted Mama to separate from Father. Veronica could not—*would not*—pretend to be happily married to a man who refused to be faithful. Even without an heir, she would not welcome such a man into her bed. Their entire future hung in the balance of this conversation.

An inscrutable expression settled on Sebastian's face and a muscle ticked in his jaw. "It's taken care of," he replied in a monotone voice.

Veronica had expelled a deep breath, one filled with relief. The riotous nerves that had made her feel as if she would cast up her accounts had settled, but she needed one final assurance. "I have your *word*?" she prodded. "You won't have *anything* further to do with Melissa?"

Sebastian's gaze had remained focused on the path in

front of them, but he had nodded and replied distinctively, "You have my word."

That—Veronica had hoped—had been an end to it. Only it hadn't been an end to it, after all. He'd *broken* his word. Barely two months into their marriage. Broken it and then lied about it. Veronica had been devastated the night Sebastian had finally admitted to going to Melissa's town house. He'd promised. And *that* was why she couldn't trust him.

He may have held her hand and said he wanted her by his side, but nothing had changed between them. He only wanted her there as a partner for social obligations. He couldn't change the past...liars were liars...there was no future for them.

# CHAPTER TWELVE

Sebastian woke the next morning to a pounding head. After he'd left their bedchamber last night, he'd made his way down to Whitmore's study and helped himself to a few too many glasses of brandy. It was unlike Sebastian to drink to excess, and he wasn't proud of himself. But then again, he'd been doing many things lately that were unlike him. Not the least of which had been to try to reason with his wife, who he already knew damn well was unreasonable.

He pushed himself up to a sitting position and glanced over to find her side of the bed empty. It wasn't a complete surprise. She'd been sleeping peacefully when he'd crawled back into bed in the wee hours of the morning. No doubt it was later than he'd expected to sleep.

A piece of paper on her pillow caught his eye. He nearly hadn't seen the white slip against the white fabric. He grabbed it and, rubbing one palm over his eye, read the curt note.

*Sebastian,*

*Please don't mistake last night for anything more than it
was. The fulfillment of a bargain.*
*Veronica*

White hot anger filled his mind, and he crumpled the
note in his palm and threw it across the room. *Don't mistake,*
she'd written. *The fulfillment of a bargain?* Did fulfilling a
bargain involve her panting his name in his ear? Did her
thighs tremble from his touch because of an agreement? Did
her fingernails dig into his shoulders because of a bloody
bargain? All this time, she'd accused *him* of being a liar. Well,
she was one too. Because it was a damned lie that she had
only been fulfilling a bargain when they'd made love both
times yesterday. How dare she act like it was anything less?

The woman had had an excellent time in bed with him
and she refused to admit it. Sebastian stood and paced across
the room, scrubbing a hand through his hair. He wanted to
punch the wall. Instead, he stalked to the wardrobe and rang
for Chadwick. He was going for a ride.

Two hours and several miles later, Sebastian galloped back
toward the stables atop Ronan, one of Whitmore's finest
horses. Sebastian was no longer angry. The brisk December
air and long ride had done what it always did for him…made
him see reason. The note wasn't Veronica's fault. It was his.

Veronica had never pretended to be anything more than
she truly was…a carefully raised young lady, who'd been
looking for a husband on the marriage mart. She was
familiar with him, since he'd been Justin's closest friend. He
was titled and rich and not difficult on the eyes—if he said so
himself. It was no wonder she'd assumed he would be a
perfectly fine husband for the type of marriage most of the

*ton* enjoyed. One of shared responsibilities and social obligations. He'd tried to offer her that life again last night. She clearly wasn't interested.

But he was the one who insisted on trying to make their marriage into something it wasn't, a true partnership. He was the one who'd put her on a pedestal, tried to make her into something she wasn't and probably never could be, a loving, trusting wife. He'd hoped for more than a shallow marriage based on family blood lines and dowries changing hands. He'd hoped for something more than what his parents had had. A loveless marriage in which his mother had loved neither his father nor himself. Sebastian had thought he'd found that different type of wife in his best friend's sister, a girl he'd known since he was young. A girl who had always laughed at his jests and told some excellent ones of her own. A girl who smiled shyly at him when they were young, and who had blossomed into a beautiful, composed young woman who met every criterion to be a perfect duchess. But also (or so he dreamed) would truly love him and be a partner...want him by her side, in her bed at night. And they'd lived in that dream for a short time. A brief time. It had ended when she'd turned on him after one mistake. Turned on him and refused to listen to his side of the story. Veronica wasn't a loving, trusting wife. She was as cold and heartless as his mother. She was just another woman who never loved him. And he couldn't blame her. The memory of the night she'd come to his bedchamber in London and asked him to join her here for Christmastide flashed through his mind. Veronica had flinched when he'd said, "You want me to come to Christmastide at Whitmore Manor and *pretend* that we are still in love?" Proof that she'd never loved him. Clearly, he was...unlovable.

He needed to stop living in a dream. Reality might be harsh, but he'd never been one to shy away from it. He wouldn't start now. He'd fulfill his end of the bargain by staying 'til Boxing Day. Then Veronica could return to the country for all he cared until the Twelfth Night ball. They could attend the event together, adept at *pretending* to be happy, and then go their separate ways once more. Neither of them with any more illusions about the other. Exactly the way it had been for the past two years.

And he knew one thing for certain, born of his anger at her note. He would *not* touch her again. Not unless *she* initiated it.

VERONICA BARELY HEARD a word Grandpapa said. He'd been speaking to her for several minutes about the gift he'd made for Grandmama for Christmas, but Veronica's thoughts were too preoccupied with what had happened with Sebastian last night. He'd been angry when he'd left the bedchamber. And he was probably even more angry now that he'd no doubt awoken and read her note. She'd been angry too when she'd written it. Angry that he'd been able to break down her defenses in so short a time and make her wild with wanting him again.

The man was a liar and a cheater. Was she such a wanton that she couldn't control herself around him for one day? Yes, she'd agreed to share his bed, but she hadn't agreed to *enjoy* it so thoroughly. She already regretted the harsh words she'd written, but it was too late to sneak back into the room and retrieve them. She heard his voice in the next room speaking to Mama. Sebastian was awake and having breakfast. That meant he'd already read her note.

Veronica had awoken early and met Grandpapa in the conservatory for a stroll through the lilies before he got tired and asked to go sit in the drawing room, which is where they were now. She intended to spend as much time as possible with her grandfather. After all, that's why she'd dragged Sebastian here. It was why they were playacting to begin with, to make Grandpapa's last holiday a special one. She shouldn't have spent so much time with Sebastian yesterday. Especially not in bed. It only confused things.

She shook her head to clear it of thoughts of her husband and returned her attention fully to her beloved grandfather. "I'm certain Grandmama will love it," she said, smiling at the thought of her grandmother being gifted a wooden box with mementos from the summer she met Grandpapa stashed inside. He had explained that he'd been going through an old box of things and found a handkerchief she'd given him with a sprig of lavender embroidered on it, a small lock of her dark hair, and a thin gold chain she'd worn around her neck the night they met.

"When you get older," Grandpapa continued, "you find you want more things that really matter and fewer things just for the sake of having things. That's why I never buy your grandmother jewelry. She told me many years ago she didn't want it."

Veronica laughed. "That sounds like Grandmama."

"And here I thought she loved all those gaudy expensive baubles I'd been buying her." He shook his head. "You know what she told me?"

"What?" Veronica asked, leaning forward in her seat to watch her grandfather's animated face. He looked so happy and…fit.

"She said she'd give them all back and then some for more years with me." He shook his head and smiled.

A sharp pain tugged at Veronica's heart and unwanted tears welled in her eyes. Before she could stop herself or grab her handkerchief, the blasted tears began streaming down her face.

"There, there now, dear." Grandpapa reached out and patted Veronica's knee. "I didn't mean to make you cry. What's wrong?"

"N…nothing," Veronica insisted as she accepted the handkerchief he'd pulled from the pocket of his coat. Even at his advanced age, the man remained a true gentleman. She dabbed at her eyes, hating herself for crying in front of her grandfather when it was her sole mission to make his holiday a happy one.

"Don't tell me it's nothing," Grandpapa said, "when it's obviously something. I may be old, but I've got two eyes in my head."

"It's truly nothing," she insisted. "I'm just so happy for you and Grandmama that after all these years, you're still so in love."

Grandpapa nodded sagely. "We are," he said simply. "But it was quite a lot of work."

Veronica frowned. "What do you mean?"

"I mean love is something you *choose* to do every day. It's not something that's just lying around like a timepiece that you can stick in your pocket and keep for sixty years."

She cocked her head to the side and stared at her grandfather as if he'd taken leave of his senses. "I don't understand."

Grandpapa sighed. "I suppose you don't." He reached over and covered her small icy hands with his large, warm ones. "Listen to me, V. Love is an action. It's something you do… something you *choose* to do. It's a decision."

Veronica swallowed. Her throat was still clogged. She still didn't understand. "Yes, but you and Mama always told me that choosing the right partner to begin with is the most important part."

Grandpapa pressed his lips together. "That's true. And your Mama…unfortunately, she chose poorly."

Veronica swallowed hard. They'd also told her that a

spouse who cheats would always cheat. They'd stressed the importance of choosing wisely. When she'd asked Grandpapa about Sebastian, Grandpapa had given his blessing. Yet Veronica hadn't even known Sebastian had a mistress until *after* they'd wed. She'd insisted he give up his mistress. And he'd agreed. But he had lied to her. She'd taken him at his word, and he'd lied to her. Just like Father had done so many times to Mama.

Veronica wanted to sob. She'd made such a mistake, and she couldn't tell Grandpapa about it now. First, it was too late. And second, her grandfather loved Sebastian. He thought the world of him. It made her heart hurt to think about telling him the truth. She wasn't entirely blameless. She should have *asked* if the man had a mistress. It had been foolish of her to assume he didn't. But she'd let her feelings for him overwhelm her reason. *She'd* made the mistake, and *she* had to live with it. It wasn't Grandpapa's fault. She'd been so afraid to have an awful marriage like her parents' instead of her grandparents' lovely marriage. And despite her fear and the care she'd taken in waiting so long to choose a husband, she'd made the same mistake as Mama.

Veronica been tempted last night…for a few lovely moments after he'd told her he missed her, she'd been sorely tempted to believe that she and Sebastian might have a chance at happiness. But she'd known all along that had been nothing but a silly dream. He was only being nice to her because he wanted an heir and a duchess to grace his arm, and she was his only chance at either.

He insisted he had not taken Melissa to bed, but what else had he been doing at her town house that night? Paying a social call? It made little sense. He was obviously a liar. And he didn't even have the grace to admit to it. No. Sebastian entirely denied that he'd cheated, clearly taking her for a fool.

"Once you've got the right partner at your side, it's up to you to keep them there," Grandpapa continued.

Veronica shook her head and concentrated on his words. She refused to allow her ridiculous problems with Sebastian keep her from spending time with her beloved Grandpapa.

"And your partner must do the same. You both must make the *choice* every day to love and to accept love. That's what true love is," Grandpapa finished.

Veronica smiled and squeezed his hand. His advice couldn't help her now. She'd already made the wrong choice, married the wrong man. Her tears had dried, but she still couldn't do it. She couldn't tell him the truth. She didn't want her beloved grandfather to go to his grave worried about her, knowing she'd ruined her chance at true love. *True love?* She sighed. It sounded quite wonderful, but it certainly wasn't what she and Sebastian had. No. It was too late for her. She'd picked the wrong partner. An irreversible mistake.

# CHAPTER THIRTEEN

The next few days passed with an alacrity that surprised Sebastian. He'd sent his footmen to and from London with some business correspondence and other tasks while using the study at Whitmore Manor—with Justin's permission—to review the ledgers he'd brought with him, write letters, and take care of other business matters. The distraction kept his mind from his maddening wife, at least.

He'd stuck to his vow and hadn't touched her since the night they'd first arrived, though he wanted her beyond reason. With each passing day, the temptation to put his hands on her grew stronger, but so did his determination. He refused to make love to a woman who wouldn't even admit to enjoying it. Even for an heir. If she wasn't with child already, he supposed some distant cousin would eventually inherit the title. At the moment, he didn't give a bloody damn.

If she wondered why he hadn't reached for her as they laid next to each other in bed night after night, their breathing mingling in the cold air that the hearth across the room couldn't entirely warm, she said nothing. She hadn't reached for him either, of course. And it was completely absurd to be disappointed by an outcome that was entirely predictable.

They were pleasant but aloof toward one another in her grandfather's presence and walked past each other like polite ghosts when the older man was not around. They remained that way until Christmas Eve.

The tradition at Whitmore Manor was for everyone to exchange their gifts on Christmas Eve. Not on Christmas Day or Boxing Day or even Twelfth Night as other households did. Sebastian had chosen his gift for Veronica with care. He'd sent a footman back to London for it that first day. Now he wondered if it was too much. But it was already here and already wrapped. He supposed he might as well give it to her. He'd also chosen gifts for the other members of the family. A bracelet for Jessica, a book for Elizabeth, and gifts for the others each carefully selected…but none as important as the one he'd picked out for Veronica.

Her gift had been hidden in his trunk in his dressing room and now, in the magnificent drawing room, with the entire family gathered, busily preoccupied with exchanging their own gifts, he presented it to his wife. They might be in a quiet standoff, but it was Christmastide and what was the sense of letting their same old fight, the one they apparently could never resolve, keep them from a joyful holiday?

"What's this?" Veronica asked, staring at the large box he handed her, a frown marking her brow.

"It's a gift for you…for Christmastide," Sebastian replied.

She glanced up at him with uncertain eyes, biting her lip. She was wearing a lovely ruby-red gown with a white satin sash along the empire waist. She looked like a Christmastide gift herself.

A smile covered his face. "Open it."

~

VERONICA CAREFULLY PULLED at the wide red bow atop the box until it fell to the sides, and she could remove the lid. Inside was a pretty, silver-painted wooden box. She pulled it out and set it atop her lap, giving Sebastian a tentative smile. Oh, dear. She hoped it wasn't jewelry. If it was, he needn't have spent so much. She'd tell him so. They'd been cordial to each other for the past several days. They'd fallen into a courteous sort of *détente* that Veronica quite relished as a respite from their constant sniping. But she still regretted leaving that stupid note on his pillow. He hadn't tried to touch her in days. And she *certainly* hadn't expected a gift from him.

"Go ahead," he prompted, nodding toward the box.

She carefully lifted the lid to reveal a set of paints in a variety of colors and several well-made wooden brushes of various sizes.

Veronica's voice caught. "Paints?"

He nodded, a tentative smile on his face.

"It's a very fine set." Veronica ran her fingers along the beautiful brushes.

"Do you like it?" Sebastian asked, biting at his lower lip, and looking so much younger and hopeful than she'd seen him in an age. Was he truly worried she wouldn't like it?

She met his gaze. "I love it. Truly. I—" She stopped. At a loss for words. Instead, she turned and pulled an emerald-green box from the tabletop behind her. "This is for you."

An inscrutable look crossed Sebastian's face, and he took a seat next to her on the settee and set the box on his lap.

"I...purchased it the summer before...er. I never got a chance to give it to you the first Christmastide we were married," she explained. She didn't want him to think she'd gone to any sort of trouble to buy him this gift recently. Certainly not since…things had changed between them.

"Oh," Sebastian murmured. He pulled off the silver ribbon and removed the lid. Inside was a black onyx panther. He lifted it from the box and examined the piece of art. It had emeralds for eyes, he noted. "It's…very fine."

Veronica glanced away from him and nodded.

"You kept it…all this time," he said quietly.

"Well, I—" The way he said it made it sound…special. She opened her mouth to say something, to deny that keeping it had any significance, but the words wouldn't come. Which is why she was exceedingly glad for her brother's interruption when Justin came marching over to the settee.

"What do you have there?" Justin asked, pointing to Veronica's gift.

She held up the box for him to see. "Sebastian gave me a painting set."

"Ah, and what did you get him?" Justin asked.

"Never you mind," Sebastian replied, standing. He gave Justin a new billiards cue and Justin gave Sebastian a box containing a bottle of oil and some fine cloths to clean his hunting rifle.

When the men were finished exchanging presents, Veronica pulled another small box from atop the table behind her and handed it to Justin. "Here's your present, Brother. Though I daresay you deserve little more than a lump of dirt."

"Why in the world would I deserve dirt? I think I've been quite good this year," Justin replied with a grin.

"You know precisely why," Veronica replied, arching a brow at him.

Justin opened the box that contained a set of mono-grammed handkerchiefs. "Thank you," he replied, with a bow. "And here is *your* gift." He handed her a blue box with a white ribbon.

Veronica quickly unwrapped the box, which contained a gorgeous hat. It was violet, her favorite color, with a tasteful white feather on the side and a wide, white bow. She nearly squealed. "The shopkeeper told me it's the latest fashion," Justin said.

"It is! I just saw it in a periodical." Veronica exclaimed, immediately placing the hat on her head, and tying the bow beneath her chin, all while continuing to study her lovely painting set, the hint of a smile on her lips.

"I'm glad you like it. You've always been one for the latest fashions," Justin replied with a chuckle.

Sebastian grabbed two more boxes from the tabletop. "I'll just be off to give Elizabeth and Jessica their gifts," he announced. "It was nice buying gifts for the Whitmoreland family this year instead of just my mother. I don't know why I even continue to buy her things. She's liked nothing I've ever presented her with. Let alone ever said anything kind to me in her life."

Veronica's head snapped up. She searched Sebastian's face. "Your mother...was unkind to you?" Her frown intensified.

Sebastian sighed and scratched the back of his head. "Yes, I suppose I never mentioned it before because I didn't want you to know that the Sinclairs weren't a happy family. But my mother is a snake. Never believe a word she tells you."

# CHAPTER FOURTEEN

Veronica stood on the balcony overlooking the white wonderland of snow-covered trees behind the manor house. She was wearing her pelisse, hat, and gloves, but the cold still found the crevices and bit her skin. She shivered and wrapped her arms around herself more tightly.

The painting set was a beautiful gift, and it was kind of Sebastian to have remembered and bought it for her. And he hadn't merely given *her* a thoughtful gift. Her sisters were delighted with their presents of a small pearl bracelet for Jessica and a compendium of Shakespeare's comedies for Elizabeth. Grandmama and Mama had been equally charmed by the bottle of French perfume and new embroidery set he'd given them, respectively. Grandpapa had been quite pleased with the humidor he received for his favorite cheroots. In short, Sebastian was more popular than she was in her family this year. It seemed as if they all had missed him.

She'd missed him too.

The thought came out of nowhere, hitting her like a blow to the gut. She didn't want that thought. She didn't need that thought rolling around in her mind, confusing her. But something niggled...the words Sebastian had said just before he'd left to give Jessica and Elizabeth their gifts. *My mother is a snake. Never believe a word she tells you.*

Veronica certainly hadn't known that Sebastian and his mother disliked each other. Though she wasn't surprised given the fact that he hadn't introduced them until the day of their wedding. But why hadn't *she* ever bothered to ask him about his mother? It was true that every time she'd tried to bring up his childhood, his family, he'd changed the subject. But she should have pressed. She realized that now. She'd never stopped to consider why Sebastian had spent so much time at their house when he was younger. She'd just accepted it as a fact. He was simply always there, with Justin. A comforting presence. But now it saddened her to think of Sebastian choosing to spend time with another family because his own was so unhappy. His mother was a snake? Veronica couldn't help but feel sorry for a boy who had to deal with an unloving mother. She couldn't imagine such a thing. And she'd uncharitably assumed that he hadn't introduced her to his mother because he didn't want her to find out about his mistress. But now she understood that he hadn't introduced them because he didn't *like* his mother and apparently his mother didn't like him. Unfathomable, but true. Now Veronica couldn't shake the idea that his mother may have lied to her. Only she hadn't lied, had she? Sebastian had admitted he had a mistress and Veronica knew for a fact that his mistress was named Melissa. The woman had written her a letter and signed it, for goodness' sake.

So why did Sebastian's words keep swirling around in her head, making her think they were important? And when had it all got so complicated? The man had lied to her. Lied and broken his word. That was a serious problem in a marriage. And one that he'd never apologized for...not that night or any night since, not even the night he'd made her cry out his name using only his mouth.

And since then...since that night. Well, he hadn't touched her. She'd laid curled in a ball next to him, wondering when he would turn to her and kiss her neck, make her feel all the passion she'd felt before, make her melt into his arms and forget they had ever fought at least for a time, make her forget everything for those blissful minutes while they touched each other. But he had never turned to kiss her. He hadn't tried to touch her. She knew it was because of that awful note she'd left him. The note she'd wished she could take back. But it was too late. And perhaps it was for the better. If she spent more nights in his arms, would she ever be able to return to her cold, lonely bed at Edgefield Hall? Wouldn't she just miss him even more? That would only complicate things. She was in the right, after all. She always had been. Even if his mother was a lying snake as he'd said, she was still in the right. So why must she keep reminding herself of that fact?

The door behind her opened, shaking her from her reverie. She turned to see Justin striding toward her. The new pipe given to him by Sebastian was firmly clamped between his teeth and he was smiling at her.

He tugged the pipe from his lips. "You've always liked the cold," Justin said, shaking his head. A black coat covered his wide shoulders, and he pulled on a set of black gloves.

Veronica turned back to look over the landscape again. "Everything looks so pristine and perfect in the snow. It makes me feel as if everything could just start again."

Justin eyed her warily. "Is that what you would like? To start again?"

She kept her gaze trained on the snowy trees. "What are you asking, Justin?"

He sighed. "Oh, nothing. Thank you again for the hand-kerchiefs."

She chuckled. "You're lucky I didn't rip them to shreds after the way you behaved at dinner the other night."

Another smile lit Justin's face. "Come now. You cannot blame me for having some fun at your expense."

"Can't I?" she asked, pushing her shoulder against her brother's.

Justin pulled a flint from his pocket and lit the pipe. He blew a trail of smoke into the air. "Tell me something. Did you follow Sebastian?"

Veronica frowned. What in the world was her brother getting at? "Follow him where?"

"The night he went to Melissa's town house. Did you follow him? See him come out?"

Veronica's frown intensified. "I can't say the thought didn't cross my mind, but no. I didn't. I decided instead to *ask* him for the truth. Adults should have conversations. I knew his answer would determine whether I could trust him."

Justin arched a dark brow. "Ah, and he failed your test. Even though he *admitted* he went to her house."

Veronica narrowed her eyes. She didn't care for Justin's tone…or his words. "What does it matter whether I saw him leave? Besides, he only told me the truth *after* I caught him in a lie."

"But you *chose* to believe he was lying about nothing happening between them while he was there?" He blew another puff of smoke into the air. "And it matters because if you had seen him leave, you would know he wasn't there long. Certainly not long enough to—"

"Spare me. I'm not a fool." She turned and gave her brother a long-suffering stare. "Why else would he go to her town house? Besides, I shouldn't have to tell *you* that some men lie."

Justin nodded sagely. Of course she didn't have to tell her brother. He'd been there, heard all of their father's many lies through the years. "I know," Justin said more quietly. "But..." He frowned and pulled the pipe from his lips again. "Wait. Are you saying Edgefield didn't tell you *why* he went to Melissa's house?"

Veronica sighed and rolled her eyes. "It seems rather obvious."

Justin cursed under his breath. "The only thing obvious is that you two are the most stubborn fools I've ever met."

She straightened her shoulders and turned back toward the landscape. "I'm a stubborn fool? Why? Because I've been angry with you for choosing your friend over your sister?"

Justin groaned. "I've told you a dozen times. I *didn't* choose sides. And I'm not choosing them now. Even though my sister has hated me for two years and my closest friend has been in the devil's own mood for the same amount of time."

"First, I don't *hate* you. And second, what has he got to be in the devil's own mood for?" Veronica scoffed.

Justin shrugged and waved the pipe in the air. "Oh, just guessing, but perhaps because *he hasn't taken a woman to bed in over two years.*"

"What?" Veronica's jaw dropped.

"You heard me." Justin took a puff from the pipe.

Veronica narrowed her eyes. She didn't believe her brother for a second. It was an outrageous thing to say. She'd always assumed that after she'd left, Sebastian had simply carried on with Melissa. If they'd had a falling out, he'd have replaced her with someone else by now. The less Veronica knew about it, the better. But now she couldn't stop herself from asking. "How do you know that?"

This time Justin rolled his eyes. "I just know. Look, the man's not a cheater. I've known him since he was a boy."

"You'd say anything to defend him." She paused. But there was something else she wanted to ask her brother. The same thing that had been niggling at the back of her mind since Sebastian had mentioned it. "Did you know that Sebastian and his mother..." Veronica's voice drifted off. She was uncertain of how to finish the sentence. "Aren't particularly close?" she finally managed.

Justin snorted. "That is an understatement. The woman is a monster. She never liked him. From what I understand, she was angry that he was born. The moment Sebastian's father had his heir, he completely abandoned his wife to the countryside. She blamed her own *son*. How insane is that? Sebastian always told me he never wanted a marriage like that. Which is precisely why it's a pity you two are so stubborn."

Veronica frowned again. "He said that? That he didn't want a marriage like that?"

"Who would?" Justin replied. "He's always wanted a marriage based on love. And he thought he'd found one until you two had your...*ahem*...unfortunate falling out."

Veronica's breaths came in hard pants, little clouds in the cold air. What was Justin saying? What could he possibly mean? Sebastian had wanted a love match? How could that possibly be true? He'd never even told her he loved her. She'd just...wished...guessed...realized she'd been wrong about it the entire time. And he'd certainly mentioned nothing about wanting a marriage based on love.

Ha. Some love. The man barely made it eight weeks before lying to her...before returning to his mistress. She shook her head to clear it of thoughts of Sebastian. Justin's words changed nothing. Sebastian had clearly been trying to win over her brother with empty sentiments. What else would he say to his wife's *brother*, of all people?

But it was more difficult to erase the thought of Sebastian's mother blaming him for his father's infidelity, for his father leaving his mother in the country to rot. Veronica sucked in a breath. Wasn't that what she was doing? Rotting in the country? Only she was there by choice, and if by some miracle she was already with child, she would love her baby fiercely and do anything to protect him from unhappiness or strife.

Her brother cleared his throat, jolting her from her muddled thoughts. "Tell me, what are your plans after you leave Whitmore Manor? Will you be returning to the countryside?" Justin asked.

Veronica bit her lip. "No, I, er…Sebastian and I are going back to London, until after Twelfth Night."

Justin's brows snapped together. "Twelfth Night?"

She nodded. "Sebastian asked me to attend Hazeltons' ball with him, to stop the gossip about our marriage. You didn't think he agreed to come here for nothing in return, did you?" Of course, she had no intention of informing her brother of Sebastian's *other* condition.

Justin grinned. "Ah, I see. Quite clever of the old boy, really. *Hmm.* I assume you will pretend you're a happy couple at the Hazeltons' ball as well?"

"That's right," she replied with a sigh.

Justin cocked his head to the side. "Don't you tire of pretending?"

She turned to face him. "What was that?"

"Oh, nothing," Justin replied. "I'll return to London with you. We can all travel together, and when we get to London, I have another gift for you…for you *and* Sebastian."

# CHAPTER FIFTEEN

They spent their last few nights at Whitmore Manor playing games, singing along while Jessica played the pianoforte, and laughing, mostly. Sebastian realized to his dismay that it was exactly like it had always been on trips to Whitmore Manor at Christmastide. Joyful and fun. He'd missed them all the last two years. He'd missed his family.

There were Christmas cakes to eat, and Christmas-themed charades to play, and even an incident with mistletoe during which Jessica had tried to insist Sebastian kiss her. He'd steadfastly refused of course, informing the chagrined young woman that her first kiss ought to be shared with someone much more deserving. Jessica had quickly got over her disappointment as she waxed poetic about the handsome gentlemen who she would meet come spring. "But how in the world will I pick which one to kiss?" she said with such solemnity, the entire family had burst out laughing.

"I should hope it would be obvious," Elizabeth drawled.

Veronica had assured Jessica it would indeed be obvious,

before sharing a look with Sebastian that made his throat tighten.

He'd quickly shrugged it off, however, and they'd had a lovely time with her entire family, including her grandfather, who seemed more fit and healthy by the day. Sharing the holiday with his family had obviously done him a world of good.

Regardless of the enjoyment he and Veronica had downstairs each day, when they went to bed each night, Sebastian steadfastly doused the candles and refused to turn to her. Even though the scent of her perfume nearly consumed him, and the sound of her low breaths made him hard. He punched the pillow with his fist and squeezed his eyes shut. He'd be damned if he was going to make love to her while she was telling herself it was nothing more than the fulfillment of a bargain. Of course, she never turned to him either. Doubtless she was nothing but relieved that he'd stopped touching her.

They stayed longer than they'd meant to, but even though he was frustrated with her, Sebastian couldn't bring himself to make her leave her beloved grandfather. It was important that she spend as much time with the old duke as possible. It would be cruel of Sebastian to make her return to London too soon. Besides, what did it matter where they slept as long as they returned to London for the Hazeltons' ball?

When they finally took their leave of Whitmore Manor, just two days before Twelfth Night, Sebastian hugged each Whitmoreland family member and somehow wished it wasn't the last he'd see of them, knowing full well it probably was, at least for a long while. An odd lump had formed in his throat.

"Have a safe journey," Mama said as she waved to them from the front door as Veronica, Sebastian and Justin all alighted into Sebastian's coach. Justin's coach and the servants' coach would follow them back to town.

"Yes, and have fun," Jessica called from beside her mother, waving one of her new Christmas handkerchiefs dramatically. "Do come back before the Season starts, Veronica. You must help us prepare."

"Of course I will," Veronica promised.

The ride back to London was awkward. The three of them had known each other since they were children, yet they barely spoke a word. Besides mentioning the weather, the delightful food they'd consumed over Christmastide, and the general look of the barren landscape, they each buried their noses in their respective reading materials for the greater part of the long ride back. Once in a while the silence was punctuated by Justin attempting to make a jest that was greeted by silence from the other two, before he shook his head at both of them and returned his attention to his book.

They arrived in London after dark. Huge snowflakes were falling all around the coach as they dropped Justin at his town house. "I'll be by tomorrow with your other Christmas present," Justin said as he hopped down from the coach.

"You really don't need to buy us additional gifts, Justin. It's completely unnecessary," Veronica insisted.

"Gift," Justin clarified. "It's just one gift...for both of you. Call it a couple's gift. And I insist," he said before bowing and bounding up the steps and into his town house.

"What do you think he's got for us?" Veronica asked as the coach pulled away into the night toward Sebastian's town house.

"I don't have a clue," Sebastian replied. He watched her carefully. He'd never asked Veronica if she would stay with him in London. He'd simply assumed she would. It was sort of an unspoken part of their bargain. And now that they'd left Justin alone at his house, Sebastian supposed she was willing. She hadn't attempted to alight at her brother's town house as he'd been half expecting her to. But she would sleep in her *own* room tonight. He doubted she'd object, but even if she did, Sebastian couldn't bear to be so near to her any longer without touching her. Whatever control he'd had while they'd been at Whitmore Manor had snapped.

When the coach pulled to a stop in front of his town house, Sebastian jumped down first and turned to help her down. She placed her gloved hand on his coat sleeve while they stoically walked up the stairs to the front door. In the marble foyer, they handed Hawthorne their coats, hats, and gloves, before Sebastian cleared his throat. "I have a few things to finish before I retire for the evening. Show the duchess to her rooms, please, Hawthorne, and ensure they are to her liking. Bring her whatever she needs."

Hawthorne, who had been properly apprised of the arrival of both his master and mistress, was his usual efficient self. "This way, Your Grace," he intoned. "Mrs. Holland and the upstairs maids have outdone themselves. I'm certain you'll pleased with your bedchamber."

Nodding, Sebastian turned toward the corridor that led to his study. Once inside the familiar room filled with bookshelves, a desk, and a conveniently stocked sideboard, he stalked over to it and poured himself a brandy. He downed the drink in nearly one gulp and then paced toward the fireplace. He'd invented the story about having something to see to before he retired so he and Veronica would be spared any awkwardness. Better to let Hawthorne and Mrs. Holland see to Veronica. Sebastian needed space. Some time to think.

It was long past midnight before he made his way to his bedchamber. Veronica's doors were closed, both the one to the corridor and the one that connected her room to his. He had expected nothing different. But he knew well that she was there. For the first night in so long, she was in the next room. His breathing hitched. He wanted to go to her, to beg her to listen to reason, to beg her to forgive him for that one stupid lie he'd told her about not going to Melissa's town house that night. The lie he wished like hell he could take back. The lie he'd been telling himself all this time needed no explanation. The lie he'd been a fool to utter in the first place. It seemed idiotic to him now, but somehow, back then, he'd decided telling her about the fake baby would have been worse than the actual truth.

But even if he'd wanted to explain, she'd been too angry and hadn't given him a chance at the time. Then she'd disappeared to the country in a cloud of fury before he'd had the opportunity to try again. Perhaps he should have written or visited, attempted again to explain...but then he'd been locked in his own fog of disappointment that she would leave him so readily, without even hearing him out. But damn it, she would hear him out now!

Scrubbing a hand through his hair, he stalked to her door. This was it. He would explain it all to her and she'd have no choice but to see reason. He'd apologize. He'd ask for her forgiveness. And then he'd take her into his arms and make love to her. Show her with his fingers, and mouth, and body just what she meant to him. What she'd always meant to him.

Just as his hand reached for the door handle, he let it fall to his side. No. That was not what would happen if he explained himself. He might have made mistakes and had regrets over how he'd handled everything, but it was *too late*. Too much time had passed. The original argument didn't even matter any longer. He'd let it all fester for far too long, and he was a fool to think he could change things now. If he made love to her, she'd be doing it out of obligation, not desire. And he could not bear that.

Cursing himself a hundred times, Sebastian turned on his

heel and stalked back to his bed. He threw off his robe and slid under the covers. He only had to punch his pillow something like two dozen times before he finally drifted off into a fitful, uneven sleep.

~

VERONICA PACED the floor in her bedchamber. The unmistakable sound of Sebastian's door closing had met her ears minutes ago. She'd stopped, frozen. Her room was as lovely as it had always been. The white bed on a dais in the middle of the space was covered with pristine white sheets and an assortment of fluffy blankets. The huge, downy pillows made her feel as if she was floating on clouds. Vases bearing her favorite lilies were set near the doorway, on the mantel, and on her bedside table. The room had obviously been recently scrubbed with not a fleck of dust present. It smelled like lemon wax and lilies and the drawers were still filled with the lavender sachets that had been there the day she moved in. She hadn't been able to take them with her when she left, for fear they'd remind her of him.

Not that it mattered. Everything reminded her of him. Not just in this house but in the country as well. She'd meant to escape him and the memories of their life together. Instead, she'd only managed to go to a place that was even more like him. Edgefield Hall was grand but efficient. Impressive but understated, just like him. She hadn't been able to resist entering the bedchamber next to hers there. The one that he would stay in when he was in residence. He'd left some things there, clothing and some odds and ends like handkerchiefs. She'd taken one from the drawer and put it under her pillow so she could sniff it and be reminded of him on the nights that seemed to drag interminably without him.

She'd gone into the nursery there, too. Even though it made her throat ache and her eyes sting with unshed tears. Mrs. Leggett had come upon her, a tender smile on her face. She'd placed a hand over Veronica's, where it rested atop the cradle's edge. The two women had stood there silently for minutes while Veronica mourned for a child who never existed. When she'd left that room, she'd never returned.

But now she was back in London. In a house that held only wonderful memories. Memories of the many places she and Sebastian had made love. Memories of the flowers he'd given her from the gardens in the back. Of the time he'd scooped her into his arms and carried her up to his bedchamber without breaking a sweat, kissing her the entire way before they'd made love in the center of his bed. She'd felt so close to him then, hopelessly in love. Even though she'd never had the courage to tell him.

Veronica scratched at her arms, feeling as if she wanted her own skin to come off, to be anywhere but in the predicament she was in now. She'd agreed to his terms. She'd agreed to spend the nights in bed with him, and she wanted him. But he hadn't touched her since the day she'd written him that thoughtless note. It was her fault she was in here alone now, unable even to look forward to a baby. The chances were slight that she was already with child. They were wasting precious time. She would just stalk to his room and tell him so. He had no right to withhold a child from her. Not when he'd promised her the chance. Demanded it, actually.

Her hand was nearly on the door handle when she let it fall to her side. She was being ridiculous. She hadn't been the one to demand her marital rights. He had. She'd pretended as if she didn't even want them. She'd made it seem as if she was giving in to his conditions when really, all along, the thought of him taking her to bed and possibly giving her a child had been her greatest dream come true. She laughed at herself cruelly and shook her head. What would she possibly say to him if she opened that door? Would she tell him she'd been lying when she wrote that note? Would she tell him she wanted him and give him the chance to throw her vulnerability back in her face? It was nothing more than she deserved. She was a hypocrite. A hypocrite and a terrible wife.

She climbed into bed and pulled the covers under her arms, but it would be a long time before sleep overtook her.

# CHAPTER SIXTEEN

Veronica woke the next morning to an aching head and a winter wonderland outside her window. She hurried over to pull back the curtains to see pure white covering every surface. The snowstorm they'd outpaced on their way back from Whitmore Manor had finally caught up to them and blanketed London in a beautiful expanse of snow, and it was still snowing.

Mary arrived to help her dress, and she chose a ruby-red gown. Sebastian's favorite color on her. Would he remember that he'd told her that once? He'd draped her in rubies and diamonds the last time she'd worn this gown. All she'd ever wanted was him, not jewels. She asked Mary to spray her with the lily perfume, also Sebastian's favorite. And she ensured her hair was caught up in a chignon at her nape, the informal but elegant style Sebastian liked best.

"How do I look, Mary?" she asked, while surveying her countenance in the looking glass atop her dressing table. Despite her lack of sleep, she didn't look tired. In fact, she looked quite awake. Why precisely was she trying to attract him? She chose not to examine that question for too long.

"Like a veritable queen, my lady," Mary replied, giving her an encouraging smile. If Mary wondered why they were at her husband's town house in London and not back in the countryside at Edgefield Hall, she didn't say a word. Mary had heard Veronica grousing about Sebastian on more than one occasion. No doubt the servant wondered what was going on. And Veronica would tell her. When she figured it out herself. Come to think of it, Mama hadn't questioned the fact that she and Sebastian were going back to London together either. At the time Veronica had assumed it was because Mama didn't want the question to seem out of place to Grandpapa, but now Veronica wondered why her mother hadn't taken her aside to ask her why she was going back to London with her husband. Had Justin had told Mama? Veronica supposed it didn't matter.

She swept down the main staircase, through the corridor, and into the breakfast room. A frown marred her brow when she realized the room was empty. She hadn't admitted it to herself, but she had hoped that Sebastian would be there. One of the kitchen maids arrived, however, and brought her a cup of tea with cream and sugar and a plate of eggs, fruit, and a biscuit, as requested. She ate while reading the *Times*, which was a delight. In the country, the news was always old, but this news was fresh, and Veronica immediately turned to the gossip pages.

*The Duke and Duchess of Edgefield are expected to attend the Hazeltons' Twelfth Night ball.*

That bit of news nearly jumped off the page at her.

*One hopes the ball will not be affected by the incumbent snowstorm.*

*Oh, my.* Sebastian was right. There *was* gossip. Apparently, the entire *ton* was awaiting their arrival at the Hazeltons' ball. Veronica bit her lip and winced. How would it be to see her old friends? She'd let her correspondence with all but her dearest lapse while she'd been in the country. There had been too many prying questions about why she'd left and when she planned to return. She'd been so worried about Grandpapa over the last several days, she hadn't stopped to consider how it would be in London. But now it was all she could think about. What plausible explanation would she give when people asked her why she'd been gone so long? Sebastian had mentioned something about telling people she'd been ill. Would that suffice? If not, she'd have to come up with something plausible and not easily disproved.

When she'd finished both breakfast and reading the paper, Veronica looked up at the clock on the nearby mantel only to realize it was almost noon. She'd spent the entire morning scouring the paper. And Sebastian hadn't interrupted her. She frowned. Where was he? In his study again? Seeing to business? Wasn't that what he always said?

Perhaps she'd go peek in on him, see exactly how busy he was. They would need to discuss their story for the ball tomorrow night to ensure they were aligned.

She'd barely started toward the study with a determined gait when she passed the silver drawing room. From the corner of her eye, she spotted a figure, a female figure. She was several paces past the room before she realized who it was...

Veronica froze.

*No. It couldn't be.*

*It wasn't.*

She swiveled on her heel, her heart beating like a drum in her chest.

*Was it?*

She took a few tentative steps back toward the drawing room and stopped in front of the open door. She gasped, then quickly snapped her mouth shut, hoping the woman inside the room hadn't heard her.

There, sitting on the center of the dark-blue settee near the window, rummaging around in her reticule, was none other than...*Melissa.*

Without thinking, Veronica marched into the room, her arms crossed over her chest. "What is the meaning of this?" she demanded, glancing around to find that Melissa was alone in the room. Where the hell was her errant husband while his *mistress* visited?

Melissa's blue eyes widened slightly when she saw Veronica, but she didn't stand. Instead, she went back to rummaging in her reticule. Veronica let her gaze slide over the woman. She'd seen her before, once, in the street near the *modiste.* One of her married friends had pointed her out. The last two years had not been kind to the woman. She had several wrinkles across her forehead and permanent frown lines at the sides of her lips, no doubt caused from frequent bouts of pouting and cajoling and whatever else it was that mistresses did.

Footsteps hastened down the corridor and the next face Veronica saw was her brother's followed closely by Sebastian's.

"Get this woman out of my house," she demanded, glaring at Sebastian. She knew she sounded like a madwoman for referring to a place she hadn't lived in for over two years as *her* house, but she wholly didn't care.

"Calm down," Justin said while he made his way to stand next to the trollop.

Veronica's gaze flew to Sebastian. The look on his face

was a mixture of disbelief and confusion, doused with a small amount of anger as he, too, eyed his closest friend.

"Melissa is your Christmas present," Justin said next as if that ridiculous statement explained everything.

"What?" Veronica demanded, wondering for a moment if she might be struck dumb with pure rage.

"What?" Sebastian echoed as he gave Justin a look that clearly indicated he was about to toss them both out into the snow if he didn't make some sort of sense out of this immediately.

Veronica watched Sebastian. His face reflected the same amount of surprise that hers probably did. No matter what was going on, he hadn't invited Melissa here. No. This was all Justin's idea. Veronica tightened her arms over her chest and glared at her brother.

Meanwhile, Melissa pulled the strings on her reticule tight and gave Veronica a once-over.

"Explain this, Whitmore," Sebastian demanded in a voice that brooked neither disobedience nor hesitancy.

"This is Miss Wilson," Justin explained. "Miss Melissa Wilson and—"

"We know who she *is*," Veronica insisted. "*What* is she doing here?"

Justin arched a brow and shook his head at his sister. "As I said, she is your Christmas gift, you daft girl. Now sit down and listen *for once*."

"My Christmas gift," Veronica echoed, her nostrils flaring and her chest heaving with indignation. She had no intention of either sitting down or listening.

"You'd better start talking, Whitmore," Sebastian thundered.

Justin smiled tightly at both his sister and his best friend before marching over to the settee where Melissa sat and putting a hand on her shoulder. "Thank you for coming,

Miss Wilson. Now, go ahead. Tell them both the same thing you told me this morning when I paid you a visit."

Veronica turned toward the door. "I refuse to listen to—"

"No, you don't, Veronica," came Justin's simmering voice, with more force than she'd ever heard it. "You're going to listen this time. Now *sit down*."

Veronica stopped, turned, and hesitantly moved farther into the room, exchanging an uncertain glance with Sebastian. They both stepped over to the settee opposite Melissa and Justin and seated themselves.

"Go ahead, Miss Wilson," Justin prompted, clearing his throat.

Melissa straightened her shoulders and pursed her painted lips. "I suppose this is for *your* edification, Your Grace," she said pointedly staring at Veronica.

Veronica merely managed the hint of a disgruntled nod.

"I sent you a letter once, informing you that your husband was at my house," Melissa continued.

Veronica nodded woodenly again, but inside she was seething.

"Well, he *was* at my house," Melissa continued, "but not for the reason I led you to believe. He came because I had written him saying I had to see him immediately. I told him I was with child." She paused and rolled her eyes, looking the slightest bit guilty. "His child."

Veronica clenched her jaw, but otherwise, she remained entirely still. "I see."

"And?" Sebastian prompted, glaring at the woman, clearly waiting for Melissa to say more.

"And it wasn't true," Melissa continued. "None of it was true. I merely wanted to get him to come to my house so I could write you and make you jealous. I had sheets tucked under my skirts. He discovered the lie almost immediately and promptly left."

Veronica remained frozen in her seat, a hundred thoughts flying through her head. "Why are you telling me this now?"

Melissa shrugged and a catlike smile popped to her lips. "I have a new protector," she said with no small amount of pride. "I no longer need His Grace's favor." Veronica didn't miss the narrowed-eyed glare the woman gave Sebastian.

"And I convinced her to do the right thing," Justin interjected. "In the spirit of Christmastide. Correct, Miss Wilson?"

"You promised you'd secure my invitation to the Markham's holiday ball next year, Lord Whitmore," Melissa replied, in a whining tone.

"Oh, and that." Justin sighed, waving a hand in the air.

Melissa stood and made her way to the door, obviously finished with her little speech.

Justin stood too and grinned widely at his sister and his friend. He bowed at the waist to them. "You're welcome. Now, I'm leaving to escort Miss Wilson home. You can thank me later," Justin announced before offering Miss Wilson his arm and escorting her promptly from the room.

The moment they were alone together in the sitting room, Sebastian turned to Veronica, an inscrutable expression on his face.

Veronica felt as if the wind had been knocked from her chest. "She told you she was with child?" she intoned in a flat voice. She couldn't quite wrap her head around it. But...all this time...all these months...she'd never imagined there'd been any other reason for Sebastian to visit Melissa. Still... "Why didn't you tell me?" she heard herself ask next.

"Because I wanted to discern for myself first if it was true," Sebastian replied in a clipped voice.

Veronica shook her head. It was as if nothing made sense any longer. "You wanted to discern for yourself if it was true before you told your wife that your mistress was having your baby?" She squeezed her eyes shut, completely confused by the turn of events. What was he saying?

Sebastian stood and expelled his breath. He drew a hand down the front of his dark-blue coat. "That's right, Veronica. That's the entire story, the whole awful truth. I kept my visit to Melissa's from you because I'd sworn to you to have no further interactions with my former mistress. And until that day, I hadn't seen her in months. Since before we courted. But how could I ignore the possibility of a child? I would *never* do that. Once I'd confirmed her to be the liar I'd suspected, I didn't want to upset you. But when you caught me out in the lie, nothing I said mattered. You didn't believe me. You can't forgive me, so what did it matter why I was there?"

Veronica stood and made her way to the window. She stared off through the icy glass at the wide, white expanse, watching the fat flakes of snow drift to join the others on the piles in front of the house. A hundred different thoughts flew through her mind at once, but the main one, the overriding one, was...she had been a completely intolerant ass. She should say something. She knew that. But...what? What could she possibly say to make any of it right? Even an apology seemed hopelessly inadequate.

The door behind her opened, and she turned swiftly to see Sebastian about to leave.

"Where are you going?" she blurted, shattering the tomb-like silence of the room.

"Back to my study," Sebastian replied. "I'll have the maids pack your things. I'm releasing you from our bargain. You no longer need to attend the Hazeltons' ball with me tomorrow night." A muscle ticked in his jaw and his eyes were shards of jade.

Veronica closed her eyes briefly. It hurt to breathe. "You want me gone?"

"You'll have to go to your brother's tonight." Sebastian's voice was flat. "It's too dangerous to return to Edgefield Hall in this storm."

"How do you know I want to go back to Edgefield Hall?" Her throat ached. Her voice was barely more than a whisper.

"Honestly, Veronica, once the storm lets up, I don't give a damn where you go."

# CHAPTER SEVENTEEN

Later that night, Veronica sat on a cream-colored sofa in a drawing room of her brother's town house staring into an empty wine glass. She'd had three glasses of the stuff and felt no better than she had when Sebastian had unceremoniously ordered the maids to pack her things and sent her and Mary off into the snowy afternoon to Justin's house. Justin's house being only two streets away, they'd hardly been in danger while traveling.

The door to the drawing room opened and Justin stepped inside. Veronica held up her empty glass and eyed her brother through the thing. "Why do so many people say it's a good thing to drink your troubles away?"

"Pardon?" her brother asked, moving over to the sideboard and splashing brandy into a glass for himself.

"It's mentioned in books, in poetry, in plays. Drinking is supposed to help one forget one's cares, but all its done is give me a nagging headache."

"You're not doing it correctly then," Justin drawled.

"Show me how to do it correctly, please," she said hopefully.

He arched a brow at her. "Care for a brandy?"

She nodded. "Yes, absolutely I care for one. Thank you."

Justin returned to the sideboard and splashed a much smaller amount of brandy into another glass before crossing the room to hand it to her. He sat in a large sage-colored chair at right-angles to the sofa and pushed his booted feet out in front of him, crossing his legs at the ankles. He took a large sip of brandy. "Dare I ask why you're here and not at your husband's house?"

"Am I unwelcome?" Veronica countered. "This was once father's home, you know. I lived here."

"You didn't answer my question," Justin drawled.

Veronica sighed. "Sebastian and I are no longer going to the Hazeltons' ball together," Veronica admitted. "As soon as the storm passes, I'll return to Edgefield Hall."

Justin's lips formed a tight, thin line. "So that's it then? You *still* don't forgive him? Even after I brought Miss Wilson to explain." He shook his head and made a disgusted noise under his breath. Veronica was fairly certain he'd cursed.

"It's not that simple, Justin," she began.

"Isn't it?" Justin said, eyeing the liquid in his glass, his jaw tight. "Look, Veronica, I've held my tongue. For two long years I've held my tongue because I knew you were angry, and I didn't want to make things worse. But I refuse to hold my tongue any longer."

He took a deep breath and downed the rest of his brandy before discarding his glass on the table next to him and standing to pace in front of the frosty windows. "The truth is that you don't *want* happiness. In fact, I'd say you've been actively pushing it away."

Veronica remained frozen in her seat. She didn't move or say a word, just listened as her brother's harsh words bounded through the room.

"Life is about choices, Veronica. You could have chosen to trust your husband. You could choose to believe Miss Wilson and trust Sebastian even now, instead you *choose* to hold on to your petty little insults and nurse your old, misbegotten assumptions. I happen to know your husband has been telling the truth this entire time. Ask yourself, why would Melissa lie now? What does she possibly have to gain from it?"

"Sebastian's mother once told me he would cheat. She told me he was exactly like his father, who was never faithful," Veronica said in a small voice. Her brother was right, of course, but still she felt the need to defend herself, if only a little.

Justin continued his angry pacing, occasionally punctuating his words with a hand in the air. "That woman never had a kind word to say about Sebastian or his father, yet clearly you *choose* to listen to her too. You want to know why I never took your 'side,' Veronica. Because you were wrong. You've always been wrong. Sebastian isn't a cheater. The fact is that you've been so worried you married the wrong man that you didn't even notice you married the *right* one."

Veronica gasped, but Justin kept going. "And I want it to be quite clear to you as you live the rest of your life alone and unhappy and childless in that vast estate in the countryside, it's because you *chose* that, Veronica. That is your choice."

Justin scooped up his glass from the side table, stomped to the sideboard, and splashed more brandy into the glass.

"Are you quite through?" Veronica said in a calm, even tone.

"I don't care if you're angry with me. You can go back to the countryside when the storm lets up and never speak to me again," he finished, waving a hand in the air again.

"May I speak now?" she insisted.

"Fine." Justin nodded and took another large sip, but his chest was still heaving, and his dark eyes continued to flash.

"If you're quite through, I was going to say that you're perfectly right. I've been despicable and I need your help, Justin. I need you to tell me how to get him back because I'm terribly afraid it's too late."

# CHAPTER EIGHTEEN

Sebastian tossed in his bed. Punching the blasted
pillow no longer worked. He was tortured. Tortured
by what had happened between himself and Veronica
two years ago and tortured by what had taken place in his
drawing room this afternoon. He'd been a rubbish husband,
allowing his wife to molder in the countryside for two years
without trying to make things right. He'd made mistake after
mistake with Veronica. There was no doubt about it. But in
the painful silence, just after Melissa had left, he'd realized
none of that mattered. Veronica knew everything now, and
there was some relief in that, but it hadn't been enough. She
hadn't said a word. Not a single bloody word. Which told
him everything he needed to know. The explanation didn't
matter whether it came from him or Melissa. It would never
be enough for Veronica. He understood that now. And he'd
sent her away because it hurt too damn much. Only now that
it was lost to him forever, did he truly realize how much he'd
yearned for her love.

Obviously, Veronica had never loved him. If she had,
would something as small as one lie stand in the way of their

life together, their entire future? No. It was time to admit defeat. The fact was, he never should have lied to her. And now it was too late. Not only had he released her from her obligation to attend tomorrow's ball, he would also free her from this doomed marriage. It would bring scandal on both of their families and her mother might prefer to wait until Jessica and Elizabeth made good matches before announcing the news, but Sebastian would grant Veronica a divorce if that's what she wanted. He'd even falsely admit to adultery if that would make the thing go more easily.

His gut churned. Although he'd barely admitted it to himself, a part of him had always held onto the absurd hope that if he could somehow make her believe that he'd never been unfaithful, she'd forgive him for his single lie, and everything could go back to the way it was. *Ha.* What a fool he'd been. None of that mattered when she didn't love him. Perhaps now he could finally get it through his thick skull he simply was not a man who inspired love. As if his mother, who couldn't stand the sight of him, hadn't made that point crystal clear his entire life.

He no longer gave a bloody damn what the *ton* thought of him, either. Abandoned by his wife? The unlovable duke? What did it matter? He could do what his father did...take a score of mistresses, lavish them with gifts, forget all about the woman whom he'd once married, so full of senseless hope that things might be different from his parent's marriage.

But even as he had that thought he knew he wouldn't do it. He didn't want a score of mistresses. He wanted only Veronica. But he'd never had her. Not really. He would have to convince her that divorce was the best option. The blasted title demanded an heir and staying married to her like this would be unbearable. Not when he loved her so damned desperately, he wondered if he'd ever be able to take a full breath without pain again. And he couldn't damn her to a solitary life of misery. She deserved better than that.

In the meantime, Hazelton and the rest of the blowhards in Parliament would have to accept that his wife wasn't at his side tomorrow night. Or any of the nights that followed. Because Sebastian intended to tell only the truth from now on. A lie had got him into one horrible mess in his life. He would not utter any more of them. He'd tell Hazelton and all the rest of them the truth. His wife had left him. She refused to return from the countryside. She hated him. They'd all find out the truth, eventually. It might as well come from his own mouth.

Sebastian tossed back the covers and lunged out of bed. Who was he kidding? He couldn't sleep. Not tonight. He'd write her a letter, post it to Edgefield Hall. No doubt she'd run back there as soon as she could, nursing her poor opinion of him. He'd tell her he'd grant her a divorce. She'd be relieved that he'd solved their problem.

He stomped to his writing desk on the far side of the room and slid into the chair in front of it. Then he pulled out a sheet of vellum and grabbed the quill from the inkpot. Sebastian took a deep breath. Might as well get started ending this misbegotten marriage once and for all.

# CHAPTER NINETEEN

Veronica couldn't sleep. Even after three glasses of wine and a splash of brandy, she was wide awake. In fact, she was convinced she might never sleep again. Justin had been surprised when she'd asked for his help. Not that he'd been particularly helpful. "I don't know," he'd replied solemnly, shaking his head, "but whatever you do, I suggest it be grand and convincing." Then her brother had retired for the evening, adding only cryptically, "When you think of something, let me know. I'll help."

Convincing, she was certain she could accomplish, But, *grand*? What was that supposed to mean? At the moment, there was a storm outside, so her grand plans would have to wait. It was just as well it was storming, however, because she didn't have any plan, grand or otherwise.

She could write Sebastian a letter, apologizing and admitting she'd been wrong. But would he even read the thing?

She could pay Sebastian a call tomorrow and tell him she would like to go to the Hazeltons' ball with him after all. But would he even see her? He'd packed her up and shipped her off. What made her think he'd take her call?

She could arrive at the Hazeltons' ball and ask him to dance. Then, she could tell him she was no longer angry with him, and in fact, she was exceedingly sorry and desperately in love with him and had made a huge, awful mistake. After all, she *was* desperately in love with him. And she *had* made a huge, awful mistake. Only the odds of him dancing with her at the ball were probably the same as him taking her call and she'd risk embarrassing him by making a scene. And that was if he even *bothered to attend* the Hazeltons' ball.

Oh, perhaps she'd simply begin with a letter. It was somewhere to start at least. It might not be grand, but it was better than nothing. Wasn't it?

Wait. She had one more rule to make, didn't she? Her third rule could be that he had to hear her out, give her a chance to explain. No. That was nonsense. He'd already released her from the bargain. He no longer cared about their silly rules.

A letter it was.

She flung back the covers and slid out of bed, heading for the small writing desk in the corner. She'd barely gone halfway when she tripped over a lump in the rug. *Ouch.* Rubbing her foot, she knelt, feeling in the dark for the lump. It didn't take long to discover that a floorboard was out of place. She'd caught her toe on it.

She made to press the board back into place when a memory overtook her. She stood again and hurried back to the bed where she lit the lamp, then returned to the floorboard. She flipped the edge of the rug out of the way and set the lamp on the floor next to the offending board. She pulled the wooden plank out of its place and flipped it over. There, scratched into the wood, were letters she'd nearly forgotten. *V loves S.* She'd written them nearly a decade ago as an extremely certain-of-herself fifteen-year-old after a night spent talking to Sebastian in the mews behind the town house.

He'd been nineteen then and had come over to play a card game with Justin and the grooms while her parents were hosting a ball. She'd sneaked into the stables to take a mount to the park while the ball was going on. Only instead of escaping with her horse, she'd been forced to hide in the darkness of an empty stall for what seemed like ages because she hadn't expected her brother and his best friend to have planned a game of cards in the mews that night. She'd been trapped there until the card game disbanded. And when it finally did, she was so ready to leave she'd hurried from her hiding spot only to rush out the door and straight into none other than Sebastian.

He'd kept her from tumbling into the gravel and she'd put her finger to her lips, desperate to keep him from saying anything to give her away. She'd pulled him back into the darkened mews to hide.

"I thought everyone was gone," she whispered.

"I'll wait with you until it's clear," he whispered back, giving her a conspiratorial grin that made her insides turn to jelly.

Somehow that one brief exchange had turned into literal hours of talking. They'd ended up propped next to each other in the empty stall, picking at pieces of hay and asking and answering all sorts of questions. He'd told her about his love of horses. She'd told him about her love of painting. She'd even admitted to him she'd intended to go riding in the park after dark with no chaperone, something he could not condone, but said he understood when she explained that sometimes she felt overwhelmed and wanted to escape her life.

"I feel like that too sometimes," Sebastian had confided.

"What do you do when you feel that way?"

"I go riding," he said with a guilty grin. "I suppose it's different for a young man, though as I say that I realize how terribly unfair that must seem to you."

"Terribly," she'd replied with a sniff. "I don't even get to do things like play card games."

Sebastian had frowned at that. "Why not?"

She'd rolled her eyes. "Justin would never invite his younger *sister* to play cards with him. Even though I'm certain I would be excellent at shuffling a deck of cards. I've simply never learned how."

"I'll show you sometime," Sebastian had replied with a wink that Veronica had felt all the way to her toes. "I promise."

A rooster crowing at the break of dawn had finally jolted them from their cocoon and Sebastian had quickly taken his leave saying, "Here's to hoping my father hasn't realized I'm gone."

The worried look on his face made Veronica wonder just what sort of man his father was. "What would he do?" she'd asked, half afraid to hear the answer.

Sebastian had shuddered. "I hope I don't find out." He'd stood and bowed to her. "Nice talking with you, Lady Veronica."

"Please don't call me that," she had insisted. "Please just call me Veronica."

That night, after gliding on air back to her room, woozy and sleepy and filled with inappropriate thoughts of her brother's best friend, she'd pried up the floorboard. Using her letter opener, she scratched her secret on the underside of the board, then replaced it and covered it with the rug. She'd been simply unable to continue without telling some-one, something. Veronica smiled to herself. All those years, the floorboard had been the only one who knew her secret.

She and Sebastian spent time together occasionally after

that, though never for as long as they had that first night. He made good on his promise to teach her how to shuffle a deck of cards. He'd even taught her several games during stolen moments when he visited Justin.

It was no coincidence that she'd not found any of the gentlemen to her liking the year she came out. Or the year after that. Or the year after that. She'd searched every crowd for the one. Her perfect match. Only Sebastian never appeared. Finally, four springs after her debut, she'd been forced to take her fate into her own hands and asked Justin to invite Sebastian to dinner. If Justin had thought something odd about her request, he hadn't said anything more than, "Capital idea, Veronica. I haven't seen Edgefield for an age."

By then, Sebastian's father had died, and he'd become the duke. She knew from the papers that he was unmarried and that night when he'd come to dinner, when she was just beginning her fifth Season, she ensured she sat next to Sebastian so she could make him laugh with sardonic comments. Then, she'd carefully asked if he would be attending the Dunwoodys' ball.

The rest of the Season had been a whirlwind. Sebastian had come to call the day after the ball. He'd brought her a new deck of playing cards instead of the predictable flowers the other suitors had sent, lining the foyer, and she'd remained smitten ever after.

Three months later, Veronica had married Sebastian with all the love in her heart. Even after the incident with his mother and their talk afterward, their first weeks as a married couple were pure bliss. In those first two months, she'd never known such happiness could exist.

And then she received the note from Melissa.

And Sebastian admitted he lied to her.

Veronica stared at the floorboard. She knew. She'd always known, even as a fifteen-year-old girl. She loved him. And

Justin had been exactly right. She'd been so worried she'd chosen the wrong man, she didn't realize she'd chosen the right one. She'd let her fear, the fear she'd felt all those years of listening to her father's lies, overtake her the moment Sebastian admitted to a lie. The fear had told her his lie was unforgivable.

But the fear was wrong. He had lied, but he didn't have a *history* of lying. He wasn't her father, and Sebastian's lie wasn't unforgivable. It was understandable once she considered all the facts. The unforgivable thing had been *her* behavior. She'd been selfish and unbending, quick to judge and arrogant. Instead of pushing her husband away, she could have sought to understand what happened. She'd jumped to the worst conclusion about him and refused to either understand or forgive.

Grandpapa's words echoed in her aching head. *Once you've got that partner at your side, it's up to you to keep them there. And the same for your partner, by making the* choice *every day to love and to accept love.* She hadn't really listened when her grandfather had said those words. She'd been far too certain of herself, far too convinced she was right and Sebastian was wrong. But now she understood. She understood just how wise those words were and just how wrong *she* had been.

Justin said she'd *chosen* to be unhappy. He was right, too. She'd *chosen* the last two years of misery by pushing her husband away and refusing to listen to him, too frightened of being wrong to realize she'd had true love in her hands the entire time. She'd used her moral superiority to reject happiness. And now it was too late. Oh, it couldn't be too late. Could it?

She stood again and lifted the lamp, carrying it to the writing desk with her. She let out a frustrated breath and shook her head. A letter was not good enough. If she were

Sebastian and received a letter under these circumstances, she wouldn't read it. She'd toss it into the fire immediately. She wasn't about to wait for tomorrow and try to pay him a call just to have him refuse her, either. She needed to go when she knew he'd be home. Perhaps she could—

Wait. That was it. The perfect idea struck her. Grabbing the lamp once more, she rushed to the door of her bedchamber and pulled it open before racing down the corridor to her brother's room. She must wake Justin immediately. She had a plan, and it was grand.

# CHAPTER TWENTY

Sebastian had been staring at the blasted sheet of vellum for what felt like hours. He'd tried to write the letter absolving Veronica from their marriage, but it all came out sounding like a lot of gibberish. Perhaps he'd do better explaining it to her in person. Only *that* would mean he'd have to pay her a call and *that* would mean she'd have to accept his call. He plunked the quill back into the inkpot and dropped his forehead onto his hand. When had it all become so complicated? A wry smile touched his lips. When he'd agreed to see his wife again and to spend nearly a fortnight with her, that's when.

He stood and turned to stare at his bed. Perhaps he should try to get some sleep. Perhaps he'd find the correct words in the morning. He'd barely taken a step when a loud thump met his ears, followed soon after by small clicking noises…at his window?

He strode over to look out the window that faced the street, but he couldn't see anything. The panes were covered in foggy ice. The clicking sounds continued. He made his way back to the writing desk, where he grabbed his letter opener from a drawer and returned to chip away at the ice on one pane. He also used the side of his arm, warm against his dressing gown, to rub at the window. The inconsistent clicks continued and when he'd finally cleared away enough of the ice to see out, he saw...pebbles. A small group of pebbles lying in the snow on the roof beneath his window. The moon was bright enough to make them out. But what in the world had that loud thump been? He pulled open the window and stuck out his head and shoulders, bracing his hands against the sill and squinting into the darkness.

The top of a wooden ladder was barely visible along the roofline in front of his window. *What in the...?* He watched in disbelief as Veronica's dark head came into view. She looked terrified and was clinging to the ladder as if she would never let go.

Sebastian scrambled onto the snowy roof wearing nothing more than his dressing gown. He slid over to the top of the ladder and grabbed her, hauling her onto his lap in one swift movement. "Veronica, what are you doing? You could kill yourself in this snow and ice." His voice sounded harsher than he'd meant it to, but fear had made it sharp.

"I...I know," came Veronica's shaky reply. Her teeth chattered and besides not wearing a hat, he realized she wasn't wearing a coat or anything other than a shift and a dressing gown herself.

"Have you lost your mind?"

"Yes," she replied, nodding vigorously. "I have."

Pulling her with him, he clawed his way through the snow back to the window and pushed her through before tumbling inside himself and closing the window to keep out the freezing air. She shivered and shook off the snow, then rubbed her hands together, watching him warily as if she expected him to toss her back out the window at any moment.

"Where did you get pebbles in all this snow?" Sebastian asked, shaking the snow off himself.

"I don't know," she replied, still shivering. "Justin gave them to me."

Sebastian stalked to the bed and pulled off a quilt. He quickly brought it to her and wrapped it around her. "Come stand by the fire," he said, gently steering her in that direction with a hand at her back. "And tell me what in God's name you think you were doing."

"Something grand?" she replied uncertainly as she tugged the quilt more tightly over her shoulders. The moment they made it to the fireplace, she leaned in and warmed her hands in front of the flames.

"Grand?" Sebastian grabbed the poker to move the logs. "What are you talking about? And where did you get a ladder in the middle of the night?"

"Justin carried it over. I needed to talk to you."

"You couldn't have simply knocked on the front door? Wait. Is Whitmore outside?" Sebastian asked incredulously.

Veronica bit her lip and nodded.

Sebastian returned to the window and pried it open once more. "Whitmore, are you there?"

"Yes," came Whitmore's unrepentant voice.

"What are you doing?" Sebastian demanded.

"Helping my sister," was his answer.

"You might have got her killed," Sebastian yelled back, wanting to punch Whitmore in the gut for his recklessness.

"First, she insisted, and I don't have to tell *you* how stubborn she is. Second, I was holding the bottom of the ladder and watching the entire time. I would have caught her if she'd fallen. Now, are you two going to make up? I'd like to go home and get a decent night's sleep."

"Thank you, Justin," Veronica called from her spot in front of the fire.

"Go home, Whitmore. You've obviously lost your mind," Sebastian called before closing the window again. Then he stalked back to Veronica. "You might have broken your neck."

Veronica scrunched up her nose. "I didn't think you'd answer if I knocked on the front door."

"You're terrified of heights," Sebastian pointed out, his hands on his hips.

"I know. But I had to tell you something right away." She searched his face.

"Tell me, then."

Her eyes met his, and that's when he realized hers were filled with tears. "I'm sorry, Sebastian."

Sebastian froze. He stared at her as if she wasn't real before cupping a hand behind his ear. "What was that?"

"I'm sorry," she said, louder this time. "I'm sorry I didn't believe you. I'm sorry I jumped to the worst conclusion because of my fear. I'm sorry I refused to forgive you all this time. I was wrong and I'm terribly sorry. And I know you don't owe me your forgiveness, but—"

Sebastian stepped forward, gently grabbed her shoulders, and pulled her into his arms. "Are you serious, Veronica?" he whispered into her hair, a mixture of relief and incredulity sweeping through him.

"Yes," she said, trying to nod as he held her. "I'm sorry I've been such an awful wife. And I'm most sorry that I was waiting for you to say you were sorry first. That's how stubborn I am."

"I'm sorry, too," Sebastian said, hugging her tightly, squeezing his eyes shut. "I'm sorry I lied to you that night. I thought I was keeping you from pain, but all it did was cause you to mistrust me. I'm sorry I didn't tell you everything sooner. I'm sorry I ever made you doubt me for one moment." He took a deep breath and kissed the top of her head. "And I'm sorry I waited for you to say you were sorry first. I'll say I'm sorry first for the rest of our lives if you'll forgive me."

"I already have," she said, pressing her cheek against his chest. "Do you forgive me?"

"Of course, my darling," he said, leaning down and kissing her soundly.

Tears ran down her face. "Grandpapa was right. Trust is the most important thing in a marriage…besides picking the right partner. And I already did that."

Sebastian didn't speak, instead he kissed her again.

"There's just one more thing…" Veronica said the moment his lips left hers.

His brow furrowed. He dragged his thumbs across her cheeks to wipe away the tears. "What's that?"

"I love you," she breathed.

Sebastian's chest exploded with joy. His chest expanded, and he could take his first full breath in two years. A smile covered his face as he lifted her in his arms and spun her around, staring at her with wonder. "I love you, too, Veronica. I think I have since that night we talked in the mews."

He set her down, and she wrapped her arms around him and hugged him fiercely. "That's the night I fell in love with you, too. I wrote it on the floorboard. You made me laugh, and you made me want to kiss you at the same time."

Sebastian furrowed his brow. "The floorboard?"

She lifted her face, a shy smile on her lips. "In my bedchamber, at Justin's house. I'll show you sometime."

He chuckled. "Well, I wanted to kiss you, too, for what it's worth. Though you were far too young for it at the time."

"I would have let you kiss me," she said, a sly smile replacing the shy one.

He hugged her against his chest again and expelled his

breath, closing his eyes and allowing the pure joy of the moment to flood through his veins.

A few moments later, she pushed away from him enough to look up into his eyes again. "My father... He lied to my mother...over and over. He never told the truth. I was convinced that's what you would do after your mother told me you had a mistress."

His brows shot up and he frowned. "My *mother* told you?"

"Yes, and until the other day, I didn't realize how awful your mother was." She shuddered.

"I should have told you about her sooner," Sebastian said, shaking his head.

"We should have told each other many things," Veronica said wistfully. "Like what sort of marriage we both wanted and why we were frightened of finding true love."

Sebastian nodded sagely. "We were young and foolish. I never wanted you to hear how horrible my parents were. But now I realize it was wrong to keep it from you."

"And I should have told you that my father was unfaithful to Mama. I was just so caught up in falling in love with you and getting married. I never considered that bad things could come from not telling each other enough."

"That makes two of us, my darling," Sebastian said, kissing the top of her head once more.

Veronica let the blanket drop from her shoulders. She stepped back and grasped both of his hands, meeting his eyes. "I'll never make a hasty assumption again without talking to you first. And I'll never leave you again."

"I'll keep nothing from you again," Sebastian promised.

Veronica gave him a wide smile before pink blossomed on her cheeks. She lifted on her tiptoes to whisper in his ear. "Will you take me to bed now, please?" She breathed against his neck. "I want you to *make love* to me."

"Yes." He nodded, a huge smile on his face. "Of course."

Veronica stopped. "Wait. There's something I must do first."

She trotted to the window, slid it open, stuck out her head and yelled into the dark, snowy night, "I love my husband desperately!"

Then she pulled down the window and met Sebastian by the bed. "Just to erase any doubt," she explained, "and to be grand." Then she pulled off her dressing gown and slid into bed with him.

Sebastian pulled her to him and began by kissing her neck.

# CHAPTER TWENTY-ONE

*London, the next night, Lord Hazelton's Twelfth Night Ball*

The Hazeltons' town house was ablaze with the light of a thousand candles. Veronica stood in front of the closed doors to the ballroom next to Sebastian, her hand resting on his arm. Pride swelled in her chest as she glanced up at him. He was wearing his finest black evening attire, and he looked so handsome her chest ached. She was wearing one of her best gowns, a lovely deep emerald satin with small white stars sewn on the bodice and hem and a matching white sash around the empire waist.

Sebastian gave her a conspiratorial wink. "Ready?"

"Absolutely," she replied, taking a deep breath and squaring her shoulders.

A footman pulled open the doors to the ballroom, and they stepped inside. The Hazeltons' butler took one look at them and his mouth fell open. Veronica cocked her head to the side and gave the obviously flustered man a beatific smile. Sebastian arched a brow at the man. "We're the Du—"

"I know who you are, Your Grace," the man hastened to

reply, clearly gathering his wits. The butler took a deep breath and announced in a loud, clear voice. "Their Graces, the Duke and Duchess of Edgefield."

Five hundred heads snapped to face them.

Veronica kept the glorious smile pinned to her lips as Sebastian led her forward into the crowd, which soon turned into a crush of people flocking to their sides to inquire after her health.

It took the better part of a half an hour to make it through the throngs near the entrance and into the ball. When they finally stepped out into an open space, Lord Hazelton was there, arms crossed over his chest, eyes narrowed. "Your Graces," he said, bowing.

"It's good to see you, Lord Hazelton," Veronica said, struggling to keep her face entirely straight. "My husband tells me you've been concerned about my health."

"Y…yes, Your Grace," Hazelton said, turning pale. "I…I hoped you were well."

"It's true, I've had an unfortunate run of poor luck these last two years. Under the weather and all that." She waved a hand in the air. "Though I must have missed you at the other events I've attended recently."

Hazelton's eyes widened. "*Other* events, Your Grace?"

"Yes, I've been back and forth from the country several times of late. It's unfortunate that I didn't see you or Lady Hazelton during any of my visits." She blinked at him innocently.

"Yes…yes. A pity." The poor man's brow was hopelessly furrowed in confusion.

"I'm so glad I am feeling well enough to attend this year," Veronica continued. "I do so enjoy your Twelfth Night ball. Thank you for having us, my lord." And with that, she and Sebastian stepped past him. Sebastian merely nodded once and said, "Hazelton," in a clipped voice before escorting his wife off into the crowd.

They had barely finished laughing about their encounter with Hazelton when a waltz began to play. Sebastian turned to Veronica, squeezing both of her hands. "Dance with me?" he whispered in her ear.

Veronica nodded, a surge of happiness and anticipation cascading through her body. They took to the floor and began the one-two-three steps of the waltz. Soon, it seemed as if half the ballroom was watching them, though Veronica barely noticed. She had eyes only for her husband as he expertly led her through the steps of the waltz.

"It's been so long," she said under the breath.

"You belong in my arms," he answered.

When the music ended, Veronica glanced toward a raucous group who were laughing and…clapping?

"What in the worl—?" she began.

When she looked again, she realized. It was her family. There, standing not twenty paces away along the sidelines of the dancing, was…her entire family…save Justin. Mama was there and Grandpapa and Grandmama and even Jessica and Elizabeth.

She hurried over toward them, Sebastian in her wake. Together, they moved away from the crowd to the hall just outside the doors to the ballroom.

"What are you doing here?" Veronica asked. "Especially, you two." She gestured toward her sisters. "You haven't even made your debuts."

"*They* came with *me,* and Hazelton wasn't about to deny *me* anything," Grandpapa said with a chuckle, resting his weight on a black cane that perfectly matched the rest of his fine black evening attire.

"And what are *you* doing here, Grandpapa?" Veronica

asked next, turning her attention to the old man. "You should be in bed, resting, and—"

"Yes, as to that," her grandfather began, a guilty look on his face.

"We have something to tell you, dear," Mama added, biting her lip.

Veronica narrowed her eyes. "What...exactly?"

"We came to see the two of you made up," Jessica offered with an unrepentant grin, looking back and forth between Veronica and Sebastian.

Veronica frowned. "What? How did you know we made up?"

"Justin sent word early this morning," Mama admitted. "We came straightaway."

"What are you saying?" Veronica asked, her gaze jumping from familiar face to familiar face.

Guilt was written all over Mama's countenance. She winced. "We waited two long years, darling. You cannot blame us for taking things into our own hands."

"What do you mean?" Veronica narrowed her eyes on her mother, placing her fists on her hips.

"Don't blame your mother, V," Grandpapa interjected. "It was all my idea."

"What was your idea?" Veronica demanded, frowning at all of them now.

A sly smile popped to Grandpapa's lips. "To feign being so ill that you and Edgefield would be forced into proximity over Christmastide."

Veronica gasped. "You were feigning it? Grandpapa!"

Grandpapa shook his head. "You've only yourself to blame. If you hadn't been so stubborn, it never would have come to this."

"I inherited my stubbornness from *you*, Grandpapa!" Veronica insisted.

"Well, perhaps it is my fault," Grandpapa said with a grin and a shrug. "But we knew you were right for each other all along. Your mother and I never would have allowed the marriage if we didn't think that."

Veronica raised a hand in the air. "If you knew all that time Sebastian and I weren't speaking, why didn't you tell *me*?"

Sebastian's lips twitched. "Because you wouldn't have listened, of course. We all know how stubborn you are. Just like your grandfather," he finished in a singsong voice.

Veronica's frown turned into a smile, and then she laughed. "Hmm. I suppose you have a point."

"You cannot be angry with us, dear," Mama continued. "We did it for your own good."

"I, for one, was a mass of nerves," Grandmama added, a soft smile on her face. "Especially when Justin started asking his questions at dinner that first night. I was so worried I'd say the wrong things."

Veronica and Sebastian exchanged a glance. "Are you telling me that entire conversation was planned?" Veronica asked her grandmother.

"Of course, my dear," Grandmama replied. "You didn't think we'd leave something this important to chance, did you?"

"You mean the heir to the Edgefield dukedom?" Sebastian asked, frowning.

"Well, yes," Grandmama replied. "But much more importantly, our granddaughter's happiness. And yours, Edgefield. You're like a son to us, you know."

Sebastian gave the older woman a kind smile. "Thank you, my lady. I cannot tell you how grateful I am to be a part of this family."

Veronica turned to look at Sebastian. "Did you know about any of this?"

Sebastian shook his head. "I'm sorry to say that I did not, but I certainly would have willingly participated had I known."

Veronica had to grin at that.

"Look," Jessica chimed in. "We all know you two have been madly in love since you began courting. Now, will you please kiss so we know you're in love again?"

"That is an excellent idea," Sebastian said, pulling his wife into his arms and kissing her soundly.

A few moments later, he let her go amid a handful of uncomfortable coughs and throat clearings.

"So romantic," Jessica said with a sigh, clasping her hands together near her cheek. "I cannot *wait* until the Season begins."

"I can," Elizabeth added from beside her twin, her arms tightly crossed over her chest. "This all looks dreadfully boring to me," she added, glancing back into the ballroom.

They all laughed.

Veronica shook her head. "I suppose I have Justin to thank for all of this as well." She glanced around. "Where is he?"

Mama glanced around too, a frown on her face. "Yes, where has Justin gone?"

Sebastian, who was a good foot taller than the rest of the company, looked over the tops of the heads of the people standing nearest to their group. "I don't see him, but earlier he mentioned there was a particular young lady he was looking for this evening."

"What?" Mama's eyes looked as if they might pop from her skull.

"What?" A wide smile covered Grandpapa's face.

"What?" Grandmama echoed, her brows lifting.

"What?" Jessica and Elizabeth chimed together, sharing a surprised look.

"A young lady?" Veronica repeated incredulously. "I don't believe I've ever known him to look for any young lady in a crowd."

Sebastian cleared his throat. "Yes, but—"

"Why didn't you tell me earlier?" Veronica continued before spinning to face her sisters. "Quickly, girls, we must spread out and discover precisely who this young lady is."

THANK YOU FOR READING. I hope you enjoyed Veronica's and Sebastian's story. If you'd like to read more, the second book in The Whitmorelands' series is THE MARQUESS MOVE. Find out what happens when Justin meets a woman he can't forget at the Hazeltons' Twelfth Night Ball. CLICK HERE FOR THE MARQUESS MOVE.

# ALSO BY VALERIE BOWMAN

**The Whitmorelands**

The Duke Deal (Book 1)

The Marquess Move (Book 2)

The Debutante Dilemma (Book 3)

The Wallflower Win (Book 4)

**The Footmen's Club**

The Footman and I (Book 1)

Duke Looks Like a Groomsman (Book 2)

The Valet Who Loved Me (Book 3)

Save a Horse, Ride a Viscount (Book 4)

Earl Lessons (Book 5)

The Duke is Back (Book 6)

**Playful Brides**

The Unexpected Duchess (Book 1)

The Accidental Countess (Book 2)

The Unlikely Lady (Book 3)

The Irresistible Rogue (Book 4)

The Unforgettable Hero (Book 4.5)

The Untamed Earl (Book 5)

The Legendary Lord (Book 6)

Never Trust a Pirate (Book 7)

The Right Kind of Rogue (Book 8)

A Duke Like No Other (Book 9)

# ABOUT THE AUTHOR

Valerie Bowman grew up in Illinois with six sisters (she's number seven) and a huge supply of historical romance novels.

After a cold and snowy stint earning a degree in English with a minor in history at Smith College, she moved to Florida the first chance she got.

Valerie now lives in Jacksonville with her family including her two rascally dogs. When she's not writing, she keeps busy reading, traveling, or vacillating between watching crazy reality TV and PBS.

Valerie loves to hear from readers. Find her on the web at www.ValerieBowmanBooks.com.

facebook.com/ValerieBowmanAuthor

twitter.com/ValerieGBowman

instagram.com/valeriegbowman

goodreads.com/Valerie_Bowman

pinterest.com/ValerieGBowman

bookbub.com/authors/valerie-bowman

amazon.com/author/valeriebowman

Made in the USA
Monee, IL
26 January 2023